Hanif Kureishi was born and brought up in Kent. He read philosophy at King's College, London. In 1981 he won the George Devine Award for his play *Outskirts*, and in 1982 he was appointed Writer-in-Residence at the Royal Court Theatre. In 1984 he wrote *My Beautiful Laundrette*, which received an Oscar nomination for Best Screenplay. His second screenplay *Sammy and Rosie Get Laid* (1987) was followed by *London Kills Me* (1991) which he also directed. *The Buddha of Suburbia* won the Whitbread Prize for Best First Novel in 1990 and was made into a four-part drama series by the BBC in 1993. His version of Brecht's *Mother Courage* has been produced by the Royal Shakespeare Company and the Royal National Theatre. His second novel, *The Black Album*, was published in 1995. With Jon Savage he edited *The Faber Book of Pop* (1995). His collection of short stories, *Love in a Blue Time*, was published in 1997. His story *My Son the Fanatic*, from that collection, was adapted for film and released in 1998. *Intimacy*, his third novel, was published in 1998. His play *Sleep With Me* premièred at the Royal National Theatre in 1999. His second collection of stories, *Midnight All Day*, was published in 2000.

Hanif Kureishi

INTIMACY

faber and faber

First published in Great Britain in 1998
by Faber and Faber Limited
3 Queen Square London WC1N 3AU
Open market paperback edition first published in 1998
This UK paperback edition first published in 1999

Typeset by Faber and Faber Ltd
Printed and bound in Great Britain
by Mackays of Chatham plc, Chatham, Kent

A CIP record for this book
is available from the British Library

ISBN 0–571–19570–9

6 8 10 9 7 5

INTIMACY

It is the saddest night, for I am leaving and not coming back. Tomorrow morning, when the woman I have lived with for six years has gone to work on her bicycle, and our children have been taken to the park with their ball, I will pack some things into a suitcase, slip out of my house hoping that no one will see me, and take the tube to Victor's place. There, for an unspecified period, I will sleep on the floor in the tiny room he has kindly offered me, next to the kitchen. Each morning I will heave the thin single mattress back to the airing cupboard. I will stuff the musty duvet into a box. I will replace the cushions on the sofa.

I will not be returning to this life. I cannot. Perhaps I should leave a note to convey this information. 'Dear Susan, I am not coming back . . .' Perhaps it would be better to ring tomorrow afternoon. Or I could visit at the weekend. The details I haven't decided. Almost certainly I will not tell her my intentions this evening or tonight. I will put it off. Why?

Because words are actions and they make things happen. Once they are out you cannot put them back. Something irrevocable will have been done, and I am fearful and uncertain. As a matter of fact, I am trembling, and have been all afternoon, all day.

This, then, could be our last evening as an innocent, complete, ideal family; my last night with a woman I have known for ten years, a woman I know almost everything about, and want no more of. Soon we will be like strangers. No, we can never be that. Hurting someone is an act of reluctant intimacy. We will be dangerous acquaintances with a history. That first time she put her hand on my arm – I wish I had turned away. Why didn't I? The waste; the waste of time and feeling. She has said something similar about me. But do we mean it? I am in at least three minds about all questions.

I perch on the edge of the bath and watch my sons, aged five and three, one at each end. Their toys, plastic animals and bottles float on the surface, and they chatter to themselves and one another, neither fighting nor whingeing, for a change. They are ebullient and fierce, and people say what happy and affectionate children they are. This morning, before I set out for the day, knowing I had to settle a few things in my mind, the elder boy, insisting on another kiss before I closed the door, said, 'Daddy, I love everyone.'

Tomorrow I will do something that will damage and scar them.

The younger boy has been wearing chinos, a grey shirt, blue braces and a policeman's helmet. As I toss the clothes in the washing basket, I am disturbed by a sound outside. I hold my breath.

Already!

She is pushing her bicycle into the hall. She is removing the shopping bags from the basket.

Over the months, and particularly the last few days, wherever I am – working, talking, waiting for the bus – I have contemplated this rupture from all angles. Several times I have missed my tube stop, or have found myself in a familiar place that I haven't recognized. I don't always know where I am, which can be a pleasurably demanding experience. But these days I tend to feel I am squinting at things upside down.

I have been trying to convince myself that leaving someone isn't the worst thing you can do to them.

Sombre it may be, but it doesn't have to be a tragedy. If you never left anything or anyone there would be no room for the new. Naturally, to move on is an infidelity – to others, to the past, to old notions of oneself. Perhaps every day should contain at least one essential infidelity or necessary betrayal. It would be an optimistic, hopeful act, guaranteeing belief in the future – a declaration that things can be not only different but better.

Therefore I am exchanging Susan, my children, my house, and the garden full of dope plants and cherry blossom I can see through the bathroom window, for a spot at Victor's where there will be draughts and dust on the floor.

Eight years ago Victor left his wife. Since then – even excepting the Chinese prostitute who played the piano naked and brought all her belongings to their assignations – he has had only unsatisfactory loves. If the phone rings he does a kind of panicky dance, wondering what opprobrium may be on the way, and from which direction. Victor, you see, can give women hope, if not satisfaction.

We find pubs and restaurants more congenial. I must say that when Victor isn't sitting in the dark, his eyes sunken and pupils dilated with incomprehension and anger, he can be easy-going, even amusing. He doesn't mind whether I am silent or voluble. He is used to the way I dash from subject to subject, following the natural momentum of my mind. If I ask him why his wife still hates him, he will tell me. Like my children I appreciate a good story, particularly if I've heard it before. I want all the details and atmosphere. But he speaks slowly, as some Englishmen do. Often I have no idea whether he is merely waiting for another word to occur or will, perhaps, never speak again. I can only welcome such intervals as the opportunity for reverie. But will I want monologues and pauses, draughts and pubs, every day?

Susan is in the room now.

She says, 'Why don't you ever shut the bathroom door?'

'What?'

'Why don't you?'

I can't think of a reason.

She is busily kissing the children. I love her enthusiasm for them. When we really talk, it is about them, something they have said or done, as if they are a passion no one else can share or understand.

Susan doesn't touch me but presents her cheek a few inches from my lips, so that to kiss her I must lean forward, thus humiliating both of us. She smells of perfume and the street.

She goes to change and returns in jeans and sweat-shirt, with a glass of wine for each of us.

'Hallo. How are you?'

She looks at me hard, in order to have me notice her. I feel my body contract and shrink.

'Okay,' I reply.

I nod and smile. Does she see anything different in my face today? Have I given myself away yet? I must look beaten. Usually, before seeing her I prepare two or three likely subjects, as if our conversations are examinations. You see, she accuses me of being silent with her. If only she knew how I stammer within. Today, I have been too feverish to rehearse. This after-noon was particularly difficult. And silence, like darkness, can be kind; it, too, is a language. Couples have good reason for not speaking.

She talks of how her work colleagues have let her down.

'They are not good enough,' she says.

'Is that right?'

It has been difficult for her since the publishing house was taken over. But she is a woman of strong feelings anyway, of either dislike or enthusiasm. Generally they are of dislike. Others, including me, infuriate and frustrate her. It is disturbing, the way I am compelled to share her feelings, though I don't know the people. As she talks I see why I leave the bathroom door open. I can't be in a room with her for too long without feeling that there is something I must do to stop her being so angry. But I never know what I should do, and soon I feel as if she is shoving me against the wall and battering me.

The boys' bath water drains away slowly, as their toys impede the plughole. They won't move until the water is gone, and then they sit there making moustaches and hats with the remaining bubbles. Eventually I lift the younger one out. Susan takes the other.

We wrap them in thick hooded towels. With damp hair and beads of water on their necks, and being so tired and all, the boys look like diminutive boxers after a match. They argue about what pyjamas they want to wear. The younger one will only wear a Batman T-shirt. They seem to have become self-conscious at an early age. They must have got it from us.

Susan gives the younger boy a bottle, which he holds up to his mouth two-handedly, like a trumpeter. I watch her caressing his hair, kissing his dimpled fingers and rubbing his stomach. He giggles and squirms. What a quality of innocence people have when they don't expect to be harmed. Who could violate it without damaging himself? At school – I must have been eight or nine – there sat next to me a smelly boy from a poor family. One day, when we all stood, his leg slipped down behind the bench. Deliberately I jerked it up, trapping his leg. The look on his face of inexplicable and unexpected pain has stayed with me. You can choose whether to do others good or harm.

We take the children downstairs, where they lie on cushions, nonchalantly sucking their dummies, watching *The Wizard of Oz* with their eyes half open. They look like a couple of swells smoking cigars in a field on a hot day. They demand ginger biscuits, as if I am a butler. I fetch them from the kitchen without Susan noticing me. The boys extend their greedy fingers but don't look away from the TV. As the film runs they not only murmur the dialogue but echo the sound effects too. After a while, I pick up the crumbs and, having considered what to do with them, fling them in a corner.

Susan works in the kitchen, listening to the radio and looking out at the garden. She enjoys that. Her own family life, like mine, has mostly been unpleasant. Now she goes to a lot of trouble to shop well and make good meals. Even if we're having a takeaway, she won't let us eat in a slew of newspapers, children's books and correspondence. She puts out napkins, lights candles and opens the wine, insisting we have a proper family meal, including nervy silences and severe arguments.

She likes auctions, where she buys unusual pictures, prints and furniture, often with worn velvet attached to some part of them. We have a lot of lamps, cushions and curtains, some of which hang across the middle of the room, as if a play is about to start, and from which I try to stop the boys swinging. There are deep armchairs, televisions, telephones, pianos, music systems and the latest magazines and newest books in every room. Most people don't have comfort, plenty and ease like this.

At home I don't feel at home. In the morning I will let go of it. Definitely. Bye-bye.

I sit on the floor near the boys, releasing the buckle of my belt when I locate it finally in the loose folds of my belly. For a change I neither pick up the newspaper nor follow the film, but examine my sons, their feet, ears, eyes. This evening, when I am both here and not here – almost a ghost, already – I will not drink, get stoned, or argue. I have to be aware of everything. I want to develop a mental picture I can carry around and refer to when I am at Victor's place. It will be the first of the few things I must, tonight, choose to take with me.

Suddenly I feel as if I might vomit, and I slap my hand over my mouth. The feeling passes. But now I could howl! I feel as if I am in a plunging aeroplane. I will see the children as often as I can, but I will miss things here. The disorder of family life: the children's voices as they sing their scatological version of 'The Teddy Bears' Picnic'; watching them watch television through their new binoculars; the three of us dancing to the Rolling Stones, the older one balanced perilously on the coffee table, the other plunging through the sofa; seeing them on their bikes, as they speed away from me, yelling; them walking down the street in the sunshine, umbrellas up, crooning 'Singin' in the Rain'. Once, when the older boy was a baby, he threw up in one of my shoes, and I didn't notice until I was in the taxi on my way to the airport.

If I come home and the children aren't here, even if there's plenty to do, I can wander from room to room waiting for their faces to come through the door, and for the world to be re-animated by their chaotic energy.

What could be more important? Lost in the middle of my life and no way home, what kind of experience do I imagine I am forfeiting this for? I have had a surplus of emotional experience with men, women, colleagues, parents, acquaintances. I have read, thought and talked for years. Tonight, how will any of it guide me? Perhaps I should be impressed by the fact that I haven't attached myself to things, that I am loose and free enough to walk away in the morning. But what am I free for? Surely the ultimate freedom is to choose, to dispense with freedom for the obligations that tie one to life – to get involved.

This confusion isn't going to leave me alone. But by the morning my mind had better be made up about certain things. I must not descend into self-pity, at least not for longer than necessary. I have found that it is not my moods that frustrate me but the depth and indeterminacy of their duration. If I feel a bit low, I fear a year-long depression. If my once-girlfriend Nina became distant or sharp, I was convinced she was permanently detaching herself from me.

Tonight my predominant emotion is fear of the future. At least, one might say, it is better to fear things than be bored by them, and life without love is a long boredom. I may be afraid but I am not cynical. I am trying to be resolute. Tonight, don't worry, I will set the record crooked.

I should, too, consider what it is I love about life and other people. Otherwise I will turn the future into a wasteland, eliminating possibility before anything can develop. It is easy to kill oneself off without dying. Unfortunately, to get to the future one has to live through the present.

While considering these things, I have thought of several people who seem to have been depressed for most of their lives, and have accepted a condition of relative unhappiness as if it is their due. How much time have my numerous depressions wasted over all? Three years, at least. Longer than all my sexual pleasure put together, I should imagine.

I encourage myself to think of the pleasures of being a single man in London, of what there might be to look forward to. My sons look up as I giggle to myself. The other night Victor goes to a bar, meets a woman with a stud through her tongue and is invited to her loft in the East End. She likes to be tied up; she has the equipment. The stud roams his scrotum, like, as he says, a slug with a ball bearing in its head. They joke about misplacing the keys. His bottom smarts.

He calls at an unrespectable hour the next day and insists we meet for breakfast so I can hear about it. I inform him that the nanny, as nannies do, has lost the will to live and that it is difficult to get a baby-sitter first thing in the morning. But at last I arrive at the café, happy to be out and to have someone bring me breakfast, rather than running about, as I normally do, with slices of toast with jam which inevitably end up face-down on the floor.

Victor doesn't omit a moment.

'And what were you doing?' he enquires politely, at last.

I sigh. Wearing an old tracksuit and drinking beer in bed, coughing, smoking and listening to a late

Beethoven quartet on my headphones.

He and the woman never meet again. Most nights Victor watches TV alone, a plate of saveloy and chips on his lap, a pickled onion or two on the side.

Another friend: a plump, middle-aged alcoholic who is an accountant. I envied his enthusiasm as he talked of the life that marriage, for the moment, was keeping him from. He had worked too hard to enjoy sufficiently his teenage freedom the first time. He leaves his wife, buys underwear, aftershave, cuff-links, a bracelet and hair-dye. He presents himself to me.

My eyes and mouth widen.

At last I say, 'You've never looked better.'

'As always, you're very encouraging,' he says. 'Thank you, thank you.'

We shake hands and off he sets for singles clubs and bars for divorcees. He meets a woman, but she will only have him in her marital bed, to provoke her husband. He meets another. You remind me of some-one, she says; an undertaker, as it turns out. My furi-ous friend replies that it isn't *her* body he has come for. He soon learns that at his age he cares far more than formerly whom he spends his time with. What he wanted then he doesn't want now. He notices also that people become eccentric as they get older, and that there is a lot of them to take in.

'Shall I go back to my wife?' he asks.

'Try it,' I say, the expert speaking.

But she regards him suspiciously, wondering why his hair has turned aubergine and whether he has had his name engraved on a bracelet to make him identifiable after an accident. She has realized that life is possible without him.

The boys have fallen asleep. I carry them upstairs, one by one. They lie side by side under vivid duvets. I am about to kiss them when I notice their eyes are open. I dread a second wind. I am a liberal parent, afraid of my occasional rages. I always regret any superfluous restraint. I wouldn't want them to fear me; I wouldn't want them to fear anyone. I don't want to break or discourage anything in them. Occasionally, though, I do want them to believe I am in charge. Soon they are leaping from bed to bed. When they make for the door, since I am too tired to grab them, I am forced to put on my 'cross' voice. Their reluctance to go to sleep I don't understand. For months the highlight of my day has been the anticipation of unconsciousness. At least they regret the passing of each day, as do I, in a different way. Tonight we want the same thing, my boys and I: more life.

'If you lie still I will read to you,' I say.

They regard me suspiciously, but I find a book, and make a place between them. They stretch out across me, occasionally kicking one another.

It is a cruel story, as most children's stories are, and it involves a woodcutter, as most children's stories do. But inevitably it concerns a conventional family from which the father has not fled. The boys know the story so well they can tell when I skip a bit or attempt to make something up. When they stop asking questions I put the book down, creep out of the room and switch off the light. Then I return to find their faces in the covers, and kiss them. Outside I listen for their breathing. If only I could stand here all night. Then I hear them whispering to one another and giggling.

Old wives; old story.

From the beginning, starting with the girls at school, and the teachers in particular, I have looked at women in shops, on the street, in the bus, at parties, and wondered what it would be like to be with them, and what pleasures we might kindle. At school I would toss my pencil under the teacher's desk in order to crawl underneath and examine her legs. The desultory nature of the education system enabled me to develop an enthusiastic interest in girls' skirts – in the material and texture, and in whether they were billowy, loose or tight, and in which places. Skirts, like theatre curtains later, quickened my curiosity. I wanted to know what was under them. There was waiting, but there was possibility. The skirt was a transitional object; both a thing in itself and a means of getting somewhere else. This became my paradigm of important knowledge. The world is a skirt I want to lift up.

Later, I imagined that with each woman I could start afresh. There was no past. I could be a different person, if not a new one, for a time. Also I used women to protect me from other people. Wherever I might be, if I were huddled up with a whispering woman who wanted me, I could keep the world outside my skin. I could stop wanting other women. At the same time I liked to keep my options open; desiring other women kept me from the exposure and susceptibility of loving just the one. There are perils in deep knowledge.

Unsurprisingly, Susan is the one woman, apart from Mother, with whom I can do practically nothing. But now, when I am certain that I am able to speak to women without being afraid of wanting them, I am not sure that I can touch someone as I used to – frivolously. After a certain age sex can never be casual. I couldn't ask for so little. To lay your hand on another's body, or to put your mouth against another's – what a commitment that is! To choose someone is to uncover a whole life. And it is to invite them to uncover you!

Maybe that is what happened with Nina. One day a girl walks past and you want her. I've examined the moment a score of times. She and I would go over it repeatedly, in joy and in puzzlement. I can remember how tall and slim she was; and then there was the jolt, the violent jolt, when we met, and met. Something about her changed everything. But I had wanted people before, and I knew nothing about her. She was from another world. After a certain age you don't want things to be so haphazard. You want to believe that you know what it is you are doing. Perhaps that explains what I did.

My young gay friend Ian liked to stand with me out-side tube stations where I would watch the flocks of girls in the summer, after I had finished work for the day, around lunch time. There were certain locations that guaranteed more interest than others. 'A picture of impotence,' he called it. With him, looks would be exchanged and off he would go, while I waited, hav-ing coffee somewhere. Sometimes he fucked five peo-ple in a day, shoving his arm up to the elbow into men whose faces he never saw. Every night of the week there were orgies he might attend.

'I've never understood all the fuss you straights make about infidelity,' he'd say. 'It's only fucking.'

'Fucking means something,' I'd reply. But what? I'd add, 'Surely, for there to be beauty there must be mystery too.'

'When there are other people there is always mys-tery,' was his answer.

Susan has already laid the table. I open the wine and pour it. The man in the off-licence said it is an easy wine to drink. These days I find anything easy to drink.

Susan brings the food in and sets it down. I glance over the newspaper. As she eats, she turns on the TV, puts on her glasses and leans forward to watch a soap opera.

'Oh my God,' she says, as something happens.

The noise presses into my head. You'd think, if she wanted domestic drama, she could look across the table.

But I am looking away, at a tree in the garden, at a print on the wall, longing for something beautiful or made with care. I have begun to hate television as well as the other media. I was young when the rock-'n'-roll world – the apotheosis of the defiantly shallow – represented the new. It was rebellious and stood against the conventional and dead. Television, too, remained a novelty throughout my youth – all those flickering worlds admitted to one room, Father making me hold the aerial up at the window on tiptoe. Every few months something new and shiny arrived: a car, a fridge, a washing machine, a telephone. And for a time each new thing amazed us. We touched and stared at it for at least a fortnight. We were like everybody else, and ahead of some people. We thought – I don't know why – that things would be enough.

Now I resent being bombarded by vulgarity, emptiness and repetition. I have friends in television. They talk constantly of their jobs and salaries, of the politics in which they're enmeshed, and of the public, whom they never meet. But if you turn on the TV and sit down hoping to see something sustaining, you're going to be disappointed – outraged, in fact, by bullying, aggression and the forcible democratization of the intellect. I am turning off; rebelling against rebellion.

A nerve in my eye is throbbing. My hands seem to be shaking. I feel hollow and my nerves raw, as if I have been pierced by something fatal. My body knows what is going on. If I am frightened now I will feel worse tomorrow, and the day after, and the day after that. All this, in the name of some kind of liberation. But terrible feelings go away after a time – that is one of the terrible things about them.

At university I met a woman as sad as me, if not sadder. For six years, before I met Susan, we lived together. To me now, that seems a long time. But then I imagined there would be time for everything. We slept in the same bed every night, and cooked and ate together. Our friends took it for granted that we were one, though at times we had other lovers. About once a month we would have sex. It was the late seventies, and relationships were nonchalant and easy, as if it had been agreed that the confinement of regularity made people mentally sick. I think I believed that if you didn't have children monogamy was unnecessary.

I want to say the smell of mimosa reminds me of her. I want to say she will always be with me in some way. But it has gone, and she is an unmourned true love.

But Nina has not gone from my mind. I am unable to let her go, yet.

I force myself to eat. I will need strength in the next few days. But no tomato has ever tasted so intransigent. Suddenly Susan touches my face with her fingertips.

'You,' she says.

'Yes?'

Maybe she can sense the velocity and turmoil of my thoughts.

'Just you, Jay. It's all right. Only that.'

I stare at her. The kindness of the gesture shocks me. I wonder if she does somehow, somewhere, love me. And if one is fortunate enough to be loved one should, surely, appreciate it. I have been anticipating an argument. That would certainly get me out of the house tonight. But I know I must do this sane and sober, and not run out of the door with my hair on fire, or while hallucinating, or while wanting to murder someone.

Tonight I want to be only as mad as I choose; not more mad than that, please.

This is not my first flight. You see, I have run away before. As a boy I would sit in my bedroom with my hands over my ears while my parents raged at one another downstairs, convinced that one would kill the other and then commit suicide. I imagined myself walking away like Dick Whittington, with a spotted handkerchief tied to a stick over my shoulder. But I could never decide on a destination. I did consider going up north, but *Billy Liar* was one of my favourite films and I knew that northern malcontents, when they could, were fleeing down south.

A few years later, one dreary afternoon, a friend and I walked out of the house and took the train from Waterloo to the coast, and then a ferry to the Isle of

Wight, where we expected to catch Bob Dylan performing 'Subterranean Homesick Blues'. All night we lay out in the drizzle in our tie-dyed T-shirts and frayed jeans, returning home the next day, disappointed and afraid. My mother was crying 'What have you done?' as I stepped back into the house. I was muttering, 'Never the same again, never the same again.'

I was right. My excursion was all round the school. It increased my standing with the hippies who had previously scorned me. They invited me to a party where I met their group – girls and boys from the local area, aged from thirteen to seventeen, who spent most evenings and all weekends together. They smoked pot, or 'shit' as it was called, and took LSD, even during classes. In the houses of absent parents, the parties were orgies, with girls and boys openly copulating and exchanging partners. Most of the children were, like me, fleeing something: their homes. I learned it wasn't necessary to keep one's parents company. You could get out. A decent teacher had shown me a Thom Gunn poem, 'On the Move', which I tore from the book and carried in the back pocket of my Levis. At parties I would lie on the floor and declaim it. 'One is always nearer by not keeping still.'

You gotta go.

Again.

After we have cleared up, Susan sits at the table writing invitations for the boys' party. Then, making a shopping list for next week, she says, 'What meals do you fancy?'

'I don't want to think about it now.'

'What's your favourite ice-cream flavour at the moment? Is it the nut crunch or the vanilla?'

'I don't know.'

She says, 'It's not like you to be unable to think of food.'

'No.'

I am considering how well I know her. The way she puts her head to one side, and the grimace she makes when concentrating. She looks as she must have as an eleven-year-old taking an exam. No doubt she will have a similar look at seventy, her gestures and movements unchanged, writing a letter to one of our sons.

How would I describe her? A characteristic image would be of her as a young teenager, getting up early to study in her bedroom, bent over a table as she is now. She would prepare for school, make her sandwiches, and leave the house, while her parents slept. She got herself into Cambridge, where she ensured she knew the most luminous people. She is as deliberate in her friendships as she is in everything else.

Though we exist at all ages at once, I can't say that I have ever seen her girlish. She is an effective, organized woman. Our fridges and freezers are full of soup, vegetables, wine, cheese and ice-cream; the flowers and bushes in the garden are labelled; the children's clothes are washed, ironed and folded. Every day there are deliveries of newspapers, books, alcohol, food and, often, of furniture. Our front path is a kind of thoroughfare for the service industries.

There are also people who come to clean the house, iron our shirts, tend the garden and cut the trees, as well as nannies, baby-sitters, child-minders and au pairs, not to mention masseurs, decorators, acupuncturists, financial advisers, piano teachers, accountants, the occasional drug dealer and people to organize all of the above and some of the below. When the numerous gadgets stop working, men come to mend them, one for each. Chalked on a board are instructions for the week, with several underlinings. Susan is always thinking of how to improve things here. She will, too, have strong, considered opinions on the latest films and music. In bed she reads cookbooks.

Being lower-middle class and from the suburbs, where poverty and pretension go together, I can see how good the middle class have it, and what a separate, sealed world they inhabit. They keep quiet about it, with reason; they feel guilty, too, but they ensure they have the best of everything, oh yes.

As with any other business, in marriage there soon develops an accepted division of labour, and a code of rules. But couples are never quite sure if they are both playing by the same ones, or whether they might have changed overnight, without the other having been informed.

It wasn't her wit or beauty that fascinated me. There was never great passion – perhaps that was the point. But there was enjoyment. Mostly I liked her humdrum dexterity and ability to cope. She wasn't helpless before the world, as I felt myself to be. She was straightforward and firm; she knew how to get things done. I envy her capability, and wish I had half of it. At the expense of feeling weak, I enable her to feel strong. If I were too strong and capable, I wouldn't need her, and we would have to part.

Susan is too prudent to want much power, but at the office she is clear and articulate. It is not difficult for her to make less confident people feel ineffectual. She doesn't know how to protect them from her stretch and vigour, and can't understand how I might see the other side. After all, she is cleverer than her colleagues, and has worked harder. Like many girls brought up to be good and well-behaved, she likes to please. Perhaps that is why young women are so suitable for the contemporary working world. They are welcome to it. Not that Susan cannot be ruthless, intent, as she has to be, on concealing her more sympathetic aspect. However, ambition without imagination is always clumsy.

Unlike me she doesn't constantly lucubrate on the splendours and depths of her mind. She finds even interesting self-awareness self-indulgent. The range of her feeling is narrow; she would consider it shameful to give way to her moods. Therefore she keeps most of herself out of view, for fear of what others, and she herself in particular, would think. I would say this odd thing. Because she has never been disillusioned or disappointed – her life has never appalled her, and she would never lapse into inner chaos – she hasn't changed.

But to keep everything going she can be bullying and strict, with a hard, charmless carapace. You have to take care with her: she will rarely cry, but she could burst into flames.

She does, too, have a curious attachment to the minor and, when permitted, major aristocracy. I don't mind a little snobbery, just as one cannot object to the more poignant vanities; they are amusing. But she does have a penchant for anyone titled, as some girls will only go out with drummers, rather than, say, bass players. I find it a puzzling attachment to a class that is not even rotting, but which is completely uninteresting. Clearly one must tolerate all kinds of irritating tendencies in others, but what of the occasions when one cannot grasp the other person at all?

I can, when I am in the mood, make her laugh, particularly at herself, which is a kind of love, because something in her has been recognized. She envies my insouciance, I think. What other function I serve I am not sure, though I have always been urgently required by her. Having had a mother who had little use for me, a woman I could neither cure nor distract, I have liked being a necessity.

But I have been pushed and shoved because I haven't known my own mind, because I have become accustomed to going along with things, and tomorrow morning we will kiss and part.

Actually, forget the kiss.

I fear loneliness, and I fear other people, I fear –

'Sorry?' I say.

Susan is speaking – asking me to get my diary.

'Why?' I say.

'Why? Just do it, if you don't mind. Just do it!'

'Don't speak to me like that. You are so harsh.'

'I'm too tired for a negotiation about diaries. The children wake at six. I have to spend the day at work. What do you do in the afternoons? I expect you sleep then!'

I say, 'You're not too tired to raise your voice.'

'It's the only way I can get you to do anything.'

'No, it's not.'

'You exhaust me.'

'And you me.'

I could strike her. She would know then. But at home we are necessarily politicians. Yet I am about to say, 'Susan, don't you understand, can't you see, that of all the nights we have spent together, this is the last one – the last one of all?'

My anger, usually contained, can be cruel and vengeful. I would willingly spill my intentions at a time like this, to achieve an easy satisfaction.

However, I should be satisfied. It is not as if I want to discover tonight that Susan and I really are suited.

I murmur, 'All right, all right, I'll do it.'

'At last.'

I shake my head at her.

Sometimes I go along with what Susan wants, but in an absurd parodic way, hoping she will see how foolish I find her. But she doesn't see it and, much to my annoyance, my co-operation pleases her.

I sit in front of her with my diary, flipping through the pages. After today the pages are blank. I have left space for the rest of my life.

'The children look beautiful at the moment, don't they?' she says.

'They are healthy and happy.'

'You love them, don't you?'

'Passionately.'

She snorts. 'I can't imagine you being passionate about anything.'

She says how much she is looking forward to the weekend away that we have planned. We will stay at the country hotel we visited several years ago, when she was first pregnant. The weather was warm. I rowed her on a lake. We ate mussels and read the papers on the beach. It will be just us, without the children, and the opportunity to talk.

'What books should we read?' she asks.

'I'll find something in my study later,' I say.

'The rest will do us good. I know things have been getting fraught here.'

'Do you think so?'

'You are gloomy and don't try. But . . . we can discuss things.'

'What things?'

She says, 'All this.' Her hands flail. 'I think we need to.'

She controls herself. 'You used to be such an affectionate man. You still are, with the children.' She reminds me that there are historic walks and castles in the vicinity of the country hotel. 'And please,' she says, 'will you remember to take your camera this time?'

'I'll try to.'

'It's not only that you're completely useless, but that you don't want any photographs of me, do you?'

'Sometimes I do.'

She says, 'No you don't. You never offer.'

'No, I don't offer.'

'That's horrible. You should have one on your desk, as I do, of you.'

I say, 'I'm not interested in photography. And you're not as vain as I am.'

'That's true.'

I pace up and down with my drink, in an agitated state. She takes no notice. For her it is just another evening.

Fear is something I recognize. My childhood still tastes of fear; of hours, days and months of fear. Fear of parents, aunts and uncles, of vicars, police and teachers, and of being kicked, abused and insulted by other children. The fear of getting into trouble, of being discovered, and the fear of being castigated, smacked, ignored, locked in, locked out, as well as the numerous other punishments that surrounded everything you attempted. There is, too, the fear of what you wanted, hated and desired; the fear of your own anger, the fear of retaliation and of annihilation. There is habit, convention and morality, as well as the fear of who you might become. It isn't surprising that you become accustomed to doing what you are told while making a safe place inside yourself, and living a secret life. Perhaps that is why stories of spies and double lives are so compelling. It is, surely, a miracle that anyone ever does anything original.

I notice that she is speaking to me again.

'By the way, Victor rang.'

'Oh yes? Any message?'

'He wanted to know when you are coming.'

She looks at me.

'Okay,' I say. 'Thank you.'

After a bit she says, 'Why don't you see more people? I mean proper people, not just Victor.'

'I can't bear the distraction,' I say. 'My internal life is too busy.'

I should add: I have enough voices to attend to, within.

'I can't imagine what you have to think about,' she says. Then she laughs. 'You didn't eat much. Your trousers are baggy. They're always falling down. You look like a builder.'

'Sorry.'

'Sorry? Don't say sorry. You sound pathetic.'

'Sometimes I am.'

She grunts. After a few moments she gets up.

'Put the dishes in the machine,' she says. 'Don't just leave them on the side for me to clear up.'

'I'll put them in the machine when I'm ready.'

'That means never.' Then she says, 'Are you coming upstairs?'

I look at her searchingly and with interest, wondering if she means sex – it must be more than a month since we've fucked – or whether she intends us to read. I like books but I don't want to get undressed for one.

'In a while,' I say.

'You are so restless.'

'Am I?'

'It is your age.'

'It must be that.'

Adults used to say that to me as a child. 'It's only a phase.'

For some people – Buddhists, I believe – life is only a phase.

*

Asif relishes the weekends. Occasionally I see the family on the towpath on Sunday mornings, the kids in yellow helmets on the back of the adults' bikes, on their way to a picnic. At university he was the brightest of our year, and was considered something of a martyr for becoming a teacher.

But he never wanted anything else. Soon after finals he and Najma married. One of his children has spent months in hospital and was lucky to survive. Asif nearly lost his mind over it. The child seems to have recovered, but Asif never forgets what he almost lost.

He doesn't often come into the city; the rush and uproar make his head whirl. But when he and I have an 'old-friends' lunch I insist he meets me in the centre of town. From the station I take him to clamorous places where there will be fashionable young women in close-fitting items.

'What a picture gallery you have brought me to!' he says, rubbing his hands. 'Is this how you spend your life?'

'Oh yes.'

I indicate their attributes and inform him that they prefer mature men.

'Does such a thing exist?' he says. 'And are you sure? Have you tried them all?'

'I'm going to. Champagne?'

'Just the one.'

'I'll have to order a bottle.'

Our talk is of books and politics, and of mutual university friends. I have had him confess that he wonders what another body might feel like. But then he imagines his wife putting out flowers as she waits for him. He says he sees her across the bed in her negligée, three children sleeping between them.

I recall him describing how much he enjoys sucking her cunt. Apparently he's grunting and slurping down there for hours, after all this time, and wonders whether his soul will only emerge through her ears. They massage one another's feet with coconut oil. In the conservatory their chairs face one another. When they are not discussing their children or important questions of the day, they read Christina Rossetti aloud.

'In five years,' he says, 'we will move house!'

When he yearns – he is not a fool – he yearns for what he has already, to play in the same cricket team as his son, for a garden pond with frogs, and a trip to the Grand Canyon. It is easy to laugh at bourgeois happiness. What other kinds are there? Asif is a rare man, unafraid of admitting his joy.

One afternoon I went to his house to pick up my children. While they played in the garden, Najma was drawing with crayons at the kitchen table. I love looking at crayons, and scrawling with them on big sheets of coloured paper. But the serenity made me uncomfortable, I don't know why. I couldn't sit still because I wanted to kiss her and push her into the bedroom, thereby, it seemed to me, smashing everything up, or testing it, or trying to see what was there, what the secret was.

Asif's happiness excludes me. After a time he and I can only smile at one another. I can't get a grip on him, as I can with Victor. It is unhappiness and the wound that compels me. Then I can understand and be of use. An atmosphere of generalized depression and mid-temperature gloom makes me feel at home. If you are drawn to unhappiness you'll never lack a friend.

If only I could see her face again. But I don't even have a photograph.

For Aristotle the aim of life is 'successful activity' or happiness, which for him is inseparable from, though not the same as, pleasure. My unhappiness benefits no one; not Susan, not the children, not myself. But perhaps happiness – that condition in which there is completion, where one has everything, and music too – is an acquired taste. Certainly I haven't acquired it in this house. Perhaps I haven't sought it or let myself feel it. Doubtless there have been opportunities. That afternoon when . . . Their smiling faces. Her hand as it . . .

Yet velvet curtains, soft cheese, compelling work and boys who can run full-tilt – it isn't enough. And if it isn't, it isn't. There's no living with that. The world is made from our imagination; our eyes enliven it, as our hands give it shape. Wanting makes it thrive; meaning is what you put in, not what you extract. You can only see what you are inclined to see, and no more. We have to make the new.

Asif has integrity and principle. Without being especially pompous, he is not ashamed to say what he believes in. He refused all that eighties cynicism. His beliefs give him stability, meaning, and a centre.

He knows where he is; the world is always recogniz-able to him. But why do people who are good at fami-lies have to be smug and assume it is the only way to live, as if everybody else is inadequate? Why can't they be blamed for being bad at promiscuity?

I have integrity too, I am sure of it. It is difficult to explain. I expect him to know my particular probity without having to go into it. I suppose I want to be loyal to something else now. Or someone else. Yes; myself. When did it start going wrong with Susan? When I opened my eyes; when I decided I wanted to see.

A few months ago we went into his study and I requested him to inform Susan that I had been with him when I had been with Nina.

He was dismayed.

'But don't ask me to do that.'

'What?'

'Lie for you,' he said.

'Aren't we friends?' I said. 'It's a sensible lie. Susan doubts me. It is making her unhappy.'

He shook his head. 'You are too used to having your own way. You are making her unhappy.'

'I am interested in someone else,' I said.

'Who is she?'

I told him little of my relationships with women; he imagined such fabulous liaisons that I didn't want to disillusion him. He said to me once, 'You remind me of someone who only ever reads the first chapter of a book. You never discover what happens next.'

He asked questions, the first of which was, 'How old is she?'

There was a discernible look of repulsion on his face, as if he were trying to swallow sour milk.

'It's only sex then.'

'There is that,' I said.

'But marriage is a battle, a terrible journey, a season in hell and a reason for living. You need to be equipped in all areas, not just the sexual.'

'Yes,' I said, dully. 'I know.'

Oh to be equipped in all areas.

After a certain age there are only certain people, in certain circumstances, whom we allow to love one another. Lately, Mother has been joking about wanting a younger man, and even looks at boys on the street and says, 'He's pretty.' It makes me shudder. Grandmother, at eighty, found a paramour with whom she held hands. She started to wear perfume and earrings. She imagined we would be pleased that she was no longer alone. How eagerly even the most seditious of us require strict convention! But Asif's favourite opera is *Don Giovanni*, and *Anna Karenina* and *Madame Bovary* his favourite novels. Testaments of fire and betrayal, all!

People don't want you to have too much pleasure; they think it's bad for you. You might start wanting it all the time. How unsettling is desire! That devil never sleeps or keeps still. Desire is naughty and doesn't conform to our ideals, which is why we have such a need of them. Desire mocks all human endeavour and makes it worthwhile. Desire is the original anarchist and undercover agent – no wonder people want it arrested and kept in a safe place. And just when we think we've got desire under control it lets us down or fills us with hope. Desire makes me laugh because it makes fools of us all. Still, rather a fool than a fascist.

When, in abstraction, I tried out the subject of separation, Asif said: 'I can just about see why someone would leave their spouse, but I can't understand how someone could leave their children. To me just going to work feels like *Sophie's Choice*.'

It is the men who must go. They are blamed for it, as I will be. I understand the necessity of blame – the idea that someone could, had they the will, courage or sense of duty, have behaved otherwise. There must, somewhere, be deliberate moral infringement rather than anarchy, to preserve the idea of justice and of meaning in the world.

Perhaps Asif will consider it all as one would the death of an acquaintance – how foolish it was of them to die. Surely it is not a mistake one would make one-self! He will shiver and feel glad it hasn't happened to him. Then he will contemplate frogs.

You sat back in your chair. It was that place we went to, chosen at random in Soho. I was looking for it this morning, to remember. Somehow I hoped you would be sitting there, waiting for me.

That day, both lost in our own perplexity, we had hardly spoken. Then you tucked your hair behind your ears so I could see your face.

You said, 'If you want me, here I am. You can have me.'

You can have me, you can.

But that was before.

The comfortable chairs, old carpets, yards of books, many pictures, and piles of CDs, create a calming silence. I've always had a room or study like this.

I read and make notes here, but I don't work at home. For the last ten years I've rented an office a bus ride away, a place as bare and minimal as they get, with, if possible, a view of a dripping stairwell. I work in short bursts, without interruption, on adaptations and original scripts for television and the cinema. I pace up and down a lot, if I'm not walking about the streets.

I am more of an engineer than an artist, although as I become more accomplished I find myself putting more of myself into the stories than formerly. I like my work to be more difficult these days. But by the time I get to a piece most of the art has already been done. It does take some talent to put the right scenes in the right order. Organization in a work is more important than people realize. If only writers in the past had seen that in the future all written stories would be translated to the screen, it would have saved a lot of time for people like me. 'Turning gold into dross,' Asif calls it.

I extract my weekend bag from the cupboard and open it. I stare into the bottom and then put it on my head. What do you take when you're never coming back? I throw a book into the bag – something by Strindberg I've been studying – and then replace the book on the shelf.

I stand here for ages looking around. I am afraid of getting too comfortable in my own house, as if, once I sit down, I will lose the desire for alteration. Above my desk is the shelf on which I keep my prizes and awards. Susan says it makes the place look like a dentist's waiting room.

An inventory, perhaps.

The desk – which my parents bought me when I was taking my A-levels – I have lugged around from squat to squat, via shared houses and council flats, until it ended up here, the first property I have owned. A significant decision, getting a mortgage. It was as if you would never be able to 'move' again.

I'll leave the desk for the boys. And the books? I can neither reread them nor throw them out. I have spent sufficient time with my face lost in a page, some of it dutiful, some of it pleasurable, some of it looking for sustenance only a living person could provide. Often I made the mistake, when young, of starting a book at the beginning and reading through to the end.

For a while I was some sort of Marxist, though I cannot any more recall the differences between all the varieties – Gramsci-ists, Leninists, Hegelians, Maoists, Althusseurians. At the time the fine distinctions were as momentous, say, as the difference between hanging someone or shooting them.

I was keen on history too: E. P. Thompson, Hobsbawm, Hill. I had an uncle who, when middle-aged, made himself 'master' Roman history, and spent years memorizing 'the classics'. Yet, at the end of his life, as well as being unable to remember a tenth of it, he couldn't even recall why he'd sought such learning or who it was for.

You might say that without a general culture nothing can be understood. But the general culture isn't getting me anywhere tonight. I can't keep my loneliness and longing away.

I must do something. But what?

And, more importantly, why?

At university I shared a flat with a friend, a handsome, intelligent man, who would sit at a table for days with only a pack of cigarettes as distraction. People might come in and out of the flat; they might be troubled or unhappy, or might want excitement, sex. Yet still he would sit there. I don't know if he was depressed, indifferent or stoical. But I envied him. Pursuing nothing, he waited. He and I discussed the possibility of living on cereal, eating it twice a day, with an orange for lunch. We discovered that one could survive on this regime for weeks without injury to one's health, if not to one's outlook. I expect to hear one day that he has killed himself.

But to be able to bear one's own mind, to wait while the inner storm of intolerable thoughts blows itself out, leaving one to contemplate the debris with some understanding – that is an enviable state of mind.

What puzzles me more than anything? The fact that I have struggled with the same questions and obsessions, and with the same dull and useless responses, for so long, for the past ten years, without experiencing any increase in knowledge, or any release from the need to know, like a rat on a wheel. How can I move beyond this? I am moving out. A breakdown is a breakthrough is a breakout. That is something.

*

One makes mistakes, gets led astray, digresses. If one could see one's crooked progress as a kind of experiment, without wishing for an impossible security – nothing interesting happens without daring – some kind of stillness might be attained.

You can, of course, experiment with your own life. Maybe you shouldn't do it with other people's.

I like walking to school at lunch-time with my long-haired sons, pulling them along and joking with them. But as soon as we enter the Victorian playground, the smell and the teacher's dogged look – her voice carries to the street – remind me of futility. If the teacher spoke to me as she does to my elder boy, I would smack her face. A braver man would take the boys home. But I drop them off and slip round to a quiet pub for a pint of Guinness, a read of the paper and a cigarette, glad it's them and not me.

I paid no attention to my schoolteachers. They had bored and scared me, unless their legs provided some compensation. But my first weeks at university shocked me into attention. I had to get home to read *Teach Yourself* books, and *The Children's Guide to* . . .

When there was no compulsion and my mind began to run, I got through Plato, Descartes, Hume, Kant, Marx, Freud, Sartre.

Philosophy was formal, abstract, cool. I chose it because I loved literature, and didn't want stories that had been poisoned by theorizing. For me that was like food that had been chewed by other people. I am ready to study seriously again – music, poetry, history. At this age, coming to my senses as a human being at last, I am not done with learning. I know I am no longer ashamed of my ignorance, nor afraid of liking things.

At university we went to the theatre several times a week, since my group of friends worked as dressers and ushers at the Royal Court, at the newly opened National, and at the RSC in the Aldwych. At the interval I would pick up girls in the audience. During the more boring plays they would slip out and talk to me. I have never found that the man being in a subordinate position has put women off. In fact, for some people, the more subordinate you are, the more 'genuine' they imagine you to be. People are afraid of too much power in others. But when I had these women I never quite knew what to do with them.

*

I am still standing upright, but something is moving and I would rather it didn't. Yes, it is me. I seem to be swaying.

I sit still a few minutes, head in hands, taking deep breaths, hoping for some deep calm. During one of our turbulent periods, Susan and I attended yoga classes in a hall at the end of the street. There were, in this class, many attractive women, most in bright leotards and all taking up adventurous positions reflected in the polished mirrors. In such circumstances I found infinite desirelessness a strain to bring on. As our souls lifted into nirvana on a collective 'oommm' my penis would press against my shorts as if to say, 'Don't forget that always I am here too!' Sexual release is the most mysticism most people can manage.

Fuck it, I will leave everything here. My sons, wandering in this forsaken room, will discover, perhaps by mistake, the treasures they need.

After school or college, in my bedroom, I would pile up Father's classical records on the spindle of my record player, and the symphonies would clatter down, one by one, until supper. It was rebellious in those days to like music that didn't sound better the louder it was played.

Then, restless at my desk, with my father's bookshelves around me, I would reach up and pull down a few volumes. Father, like the other neighbourhood men, spent most of his days' energy in unsatisfying work. Time was precious and he had me fear its waste. But browsing and ruminating at my desk, I figured that doing nothing was often the best way of doing something.

I will regret forfeiting this room. For though I have never been taught the art of solitude, but had to learn it, it has become as necessary to me as the Beatles, kisses on the back of my neck and kindness. Here I can follow the momentum of my thoughts as I read, write, sing, dance, think of the past and waste time. Here I have examined dimly felt intuitions, and captured unclear but pressing ideas. I am speaking of the pleasures of not speaking, doing or wanting, but of losing oneself.

But it was in this room, late at night, when she and the children were asleep and I sat here listening to the street, that I saw how I yearned for contact and nourishment. I never found a way to be pleasurably idle with Susan. She has a busy mind. One might want to admire anyone who lives with vigour and spirit. But there is desperation in her activity, as if her work is holding her together. In some ways, it is less of everything that I want.

I know how necessary fathers are for boys. I would hang on to Dad's hand as he toured the bookshops, climbing ladders and standing on steps to pull down rotting tomes. 'Let's go, let's go . . .' I'd say.

How utterly the past suffuses us. We live in all our days at once. The writers Dad preferred are still my favourites, mostly nineteenth-century Europeans, the Russians in particular. The characters, Goriot, Vronsky, Madame Ranevskaya, Nana, Julien Sorel, feel part of me. It is Father's copies I will give to the boys. Father took me to see war films and cricket. Whenever I appeared in his room his face would brighten. He loved kissing me. We kept one another company for years. He, more than anyone, was the person I wanted to marry. I wanted to walk, talk, laugh and dress like him. My sons are the same with me, repeating my phrases in their tiny voices, staring admiringly at me and fighting to sit beside me. But I am leaving them. What would Father think of that?

What embarrassed Nina about me embarrassed me about him. I don't yet read the newspapers wearing gloves, as Father did to prevent his fingers getting soiled. But I know many local shopkeepers, and I do bang on their windows as I pass, and will stop and ask them personal questions about the minutiae of their lives. Father would invite in any passing religious freak with a shopping bag full of pamphlets and engage in a ferocious debate.

But I lack his kindness. Of all the virtues it is the sweetest, particularly since it isn't considered a moral attribute, but as a gift. Nina always said that I am kind; she said I was the perfect man for her, and that I had everything she could want. Would she still say that?

My younger son, his nose in my wrist as we walked in the street last week, said, 'Daddy, you smell of you.'

Cheerio, I must be going.

Father, six years dead, would have been horrified by my skulking off. Such an abandonment would have seemed undignified at the very least. Susan used to go to him when we were fighting and he would take her side, phoning me and saying, 'Don't be cruel, boy.' He said she was 'all in one'. She had everything I could want. Dad left his own mother at twenty-one and never saw her again. He didn't approve of leaving, and he liked to be chivalrous. He didn't see that the women could take care of themselves. The man had the power and had to be protective.

Father believed, too, in loyalty. For him to be accused of disloyalty would have been like being called a thief. But what would he have been loyal to? After all, when required, one can always find something to attach one's stubborn faith to. Probably he would have been loyal to the idea of loyalty itself, for fear that without it the world would have been robbed of compassion, and oneself exposed.

Father was a civil servant who later worked as a clerk at Scotland Yard, for the police. In the mornings, and at weekends, he wrote novels. He must have completed five or six. A couple of them were admired by publishers, but none of them got into print. They weren't very bad and they weren't very good. He never gave up; it was all he ever wanted to do. The book on his bedside table had, on the cover, a picture of a middle-aged writer sitting on a pile of books, a portable typewriter on his knee. It was *Call It Experi-*

ence by Erskine Caldwell. Under the author's name it said, 'Reveals the secrets of a great writer's private life and literary success.' The writer did look experienced; he had been around, but he was ready to go on. He was tough. That's what a writer was.

Failure strengthened Father's resolve. He was both brave and foolish, I'd say. He wanted me to be a doctor, and I did consider it, but probably only because I was an admirer of Chekhov and Father liked Somerset Maugham. In the end Dad told me it was hopeless to take up something that wasn't going to provide me with pleasure for the rest of my life. He was wise in that way. I was adept and successful a couple of years after I left university. I could do it; I just could. Whether it was a knack or trick or talent, I didn't know. It puzzled both of us. Art is easy for those who can do it, and impossible for those who can't.

What did Father's life show me? That life is a struggle, and that struggle gets you nowhere and is neither recognized nor rewarded. There is little pleasure in marriage; it involves considerable endurance, like doing a job one hates. You can't leave and you can't enjoy it. Both he and Mother were frustrated, neither being able to find a way to get what they wanted, whatever that was. Nevertheless they were loyal and faithful to one another. Disloyal and unfaithful to themselves. Or do I misunderstand?

I run my hand down the CDs piled on every available surface. Classical, of all periods, with dark Beethoven my God; jazz, mostly of the fifties; blues, rock-'n'-roll and pop, with the emphasis on the mid-sixties and early seventies. A lot of punk. It was the hatred, I think, that appealed. It is great music but you wouldn't want to listen to it.

Victor doesn't have much music over there, and few books. He only had the Bible in his house, and no one read it, not even the Song of Solomon. Now I accompany him to record shops and he flips through the CDs. 'Who's this? What's this?' he goes.

He has a lovely helplessness, and has caught my enthusiasm. I took him to see my friend who has a shop. He bought a sky-blue suit which certainly shocks but does not outrage, except in certain low dives. He has tinted his hair. He might resemble a badger, and I did balk at the earring. But I keep my mirth down, and would say: any advance in wisdom requires a good dose of shamelessness.

Separation wouldn't have occurred to a lower-middle-class couple in the fifties. My parents remained in the same house all their lives. Mother was only partially there. Most of the day she sat, inert and obese, in her chair. She hardly spoke – except to dispute; she never touched anyone, and often wept, hating herself and all of us: a lump of living death. She wouldn't wash; there were cobwebs in all the rooms; the plates and cutlery were greasy. We hardly changed our clothes. All effort was a trouble and she lived on the edge of panic, as if everything was about to break down. Occasionally there were reminders of life, a smile or joke, even a conversation. But these were rare, and she was gone. For a long time I had the strange feeling that she reminded me of someone I used to know.

She was aware of it, in some way.

'Selfish,' she called herself, because her mind hurt so much she could only think of herself. She didn't know how to enjoy other people, the world, or her own body. I was afraid to approach her, since with such a mother you never knew whether she would send you away or put out her arms for a kiss. My existence was a disturbance. Being a burden, or interruption, I couldn't ask her for anything. But if she didn't like me, I did cause her to worry. And I worried about her worrying. Anxiety handcuffed us to one another. At least we had something in common.

When I was nominated for the Oscar and I rang to tell her, she said, 'Will you have to go all that way to America? It's a long way.'

'Thanks for the concern,' I said.

When we were older money was short. Father refused to look for another job and he wouldn't move to a different part of the country. Nothing was allowed to happen until he 'made it'. Mother was forced to find employment. She was a school dinner lady; she worked in factories and offices; she worked in a shop. I think the compulsion and other people were better for her than sitting at home.

The day I started to live with my sad girlfriend in London, I went home to pick up my things. I imagined it would be the first and last time I would leave home. I didn't know I'd be making a habit of it. My parents sat in separate armchairs, watching me carry out my records. What was there left for them to do? Hadn't I rendered them irrelevant?

But when my brother and I left, our parents started going to art galleries, to the cinema, for walks and on long holidays. They took a new interest in one another, and couldn't get enough of life. Victor says that once the lights on a love have dimmed, you can never illuminate them again, any more than you can reheat a soufflé. But my parents went through the darkness and discovered a new intimacy.

Can't you, then, apply yourself? Susan often accuses me of lack of application. It was what my teachers said, that I didn't concentrate. But I *was* concentrating. I believe the mind is always concentrated – on something that interests it. Skirts and jokes and cricket and pop, in my case. Despite ourselves, we know what we like, and our errors and distracted excursions are illuminations. Perhaps only the unsought is worthwhile – like Nina's face and the caresses of her long fingers.

Not loving Susan I insist on seeing as a weakness, as my failure and my responsibility. But what is the point of leaving if this failure reproduces itself with every woman? Suppose it is like an illness that you give to everyone you meet? Wouldn't I have to keep a bag permanently packed by any door I had taken refuge behind?

I don't want to think of that.

My bag sits on the floor.

I will be needing pens and paper on my journey. I won't want to forfeit any important emotion. I will pursue my feelings like a detective, looking for clues to the crime, writing as I read myself within. I want an absolute honesty that doesn't merely involve saying how awful one is. How do I like to write? With a soft pencil and a hard dick – not the other way round.

I like paper of all kinds: creamy, white, yellow; thick, thin, lined, plain. In my cupboard I have at least fifty notebooks, each of which, at the time of purchase, filled me with the excitement of what might be said, of new thoughts discovered. Each has a sheet of white blotting paper between the leaves, and all are blank apart from the first page, on which I have usually written something like, 'In this notebook I will write whatever comes into my mind, and after a time I will see a picture of myself emerge, made up of significant fragments . . .' And then – nothing. I freeze, as one does when things are getting illegitimately interesting.

I have tried devoting each notebook to a different subject: books I'm reading, thoughts on politics, problems I have with Mother, Susan, present lovers, etc. But as I begin, I become busy washing my weeping fountain pens, refilling them, testing the nibs and wondering why the flow isn't regular. There are few more exquisite instruments than a fountain pen as it glides over good paper, like a finger over young skin.

But somehow I am made for ferocious, uncontrolled scribbling on scrap paper with old Biros and stubby soft pencils.

For our homework, as kids, we would sometimes be asked to write, 'What I did today.' Now I feel like compiling a list: the things I didn't do today. The things I haven't done in life.

I think of the people I know (later I might write their names in a suitable notebook) and wonder which of them knows how to live well. If living is an art it is a strange one, an art of everything, and particularly of spirited pleasure. Its developed form would involve a number of qualities sewn together: intelligence, charm, good fortune, unforced virtue, along with wisdom, taste, knowledge, understanding, and the recognition of anguish and conflict as part of life. Wealth wouldn't be essential, but the intelligence to accumulate it where necessary might be. The people I can think of who live with talent are the ones who have free lives, conceiving of great schemes and seeing them fulfilled. They are, too, the best company.

Victor and I were in our favourite bar the other day, watching football on television. He said, 'When I think of how my wife and I stayed together all those barren and arduous nights and years, I cannot understand it at all. Perhaps it was a kind of mad idealism. I had made a promise that I had to fulfil at all costs. But why? The world couldn't possibly recover from the end of my marriage. My faith in everything would be shattered. I believed in it without knowing how much I believed in it. It was blind, foolish obedience and submission. Probably it was the only kind of religious faith I've had. I used to think I had some radicalism in me, but I couldn't smash the thing that bound me the most. Smash it? I couldn't even see it!'

Dear God, teach me to be careless.

*

Come on. Forward.

What do runaways wear? This is important. I should make a list, as Susan has taught me. At Victor's there will be no proper place for my clothes. I am quite fastidious about such things. It would be better to leave most of them here. But if Susan has any flair she will slash my Vivienne Westwood jacket. It would be dispiriting if my departure went unnoticed – a measure of delirium is essential. As for shoes, I can't take many pairs, but I will require something both stylish and comfortable to give myself confidence.

I have several suits, each of which I favour at different times and like to wear out to lunch, an event I look forward to all morning, since it is the first time in the day that I become aware of other people. This week I fancy the double-breasted four-button pinstripe. The trousers are tapered, with flat front pockets. I wear them with dark blue suede loafers. It's not boxy but wearing it makes me feel magisterial. I am convinced I will be served first in shops and that I can talk down to people. I will need it for all the bars and restaurants I will be visiting with Victor, to offset his sky-blue number. But I can't go round like that every day. I will need other clothes too.

I bought a brown checked suit the other day, a light, summer thing, to cheer myself up. It has to be altered and they won't send it over for a few days. I bought shirts too, but I can't remember how many or in what colours. I can't stay here just for that; I will have to ring the shop and get the stuff diverted. I can't even wear it yet. And by the time the weather has turned warmer, I will have been gone a while.

I remove my signed photograph of John Lennon from the wall and slip it into the empty bag. That is something to take. A handful of CDs too. Alfred Brendel or Emil Gilels? Marvin Gaye or Otis Redding? Perhaps I should remind myself that I am absconding, not appearing on *Desert Island Discs*. Yet I still can't hear the beginning of 'Stray Cat Blues' without wanting to hitchhike to Spain with a teenager. I am, too, more likely to listen to Hot Rats than I am to read Sartre, Camus, Ionesco, Beckett and the other poets of solitude and dread that restored me as a young man. Probably it is the human condition that we are ultimately isolated, and will die alone. But tonight, standing here, I want so much to reach out that I could punch through the window.

Patience is a virtue only in children and the imprisoned. Neither Susan nor I are impulsive. In the middle-class way, while others were frolicking and wasting – how I envied any prolonged dissipation! – we both planned and contained our frivolity in order to get all we have. I had a teacher who used to say that every extra year of education adds five thousand pounds to your income for life. I have been able to rise at five, leave the house and get to my desk by five-forty-five. I have excelled at relinquishing things I liked – it isn't any fun giving up things that are not fun. When unnerved I start seeking pleasures to relinquish. But Victor – or is it his therapist, it is easy to confuse those conspirators these days – says toleration can become a bad habit. Yes, I will defer deferral. I am getting on with it. I want it now!

I have been drinking. I will put down the beer bottle, after this swig.

How little directness there is, when you look around! We have to make things distinct by indirection. What a redundant and fearful dance it all is, as if our feelings are weapons that could kill, and words are their bullets. I will go upstairs, sit on the edge of the bed, and tell Susan firmly and truthfully that I am going to leave. I can't stay here another night. What's the point? How absurd to think that this is something one could prepare for! There is only the unknown and my coming to terms with it. I will pack, kiss the children, and go! It will be done and I will be away.

Yes!

My children hunt through their toy boxes, chucking aside the once-cherished to drag out what they need to keep themselves interested. I am the same with books, music, pictures, newspapers. Can we do this with people? That would be considered shallow. We must treat other people as if they were real. But are they?

Yet what makes me think I should have what I want? Surely you can't constantly be replacing people who don't provide what you need? There must be other opportunities for sustenance – in pictures, books, dance – even within. Yet all these forms are enraptured by love and desire, and are created from them.

Susan, who is four years younger than me, thinks we live in a selfish age. She talks of a Thatcherism of the soul that imagines that people are not dependent on one another. In love, these days, it is a free market; browse and buy, pick and choose, rent and reject, as you like. There's no sexual and social security; everyone has to take care of themselves, or not. Fulfilment, self-expression and 'creativity' are the only values.

Susan would say that we require other social forms. What are they? Probably the unpleasant ones: duty, sacrifice, obligation to others, self-discipline.

When she says such things I wonder if we haven't been a particularly privileged and spoilt generation. Between the deprivation of the post-war slump, and the cruelties of the eighties, we were the children of innocent consumerism and the inheritors of the freedoms won by our seditious elders in the late sixties. We had a free, superior and somewhat lazy education. Then we went on the dole for five years in order to pursue our self-righteous politics, before starting work in the media and making a lot of money. We weren't much restrained by morality or religion. Music, dancing and conscienceless fucking were our totems. We boasted that we were the freest there'd ever been.

Like the hippies we disdained materialism. Yet we were less frivolous than the original 'heads'. If we dropped out to become carpenters and gardeners it was because we wanted to share the experience of the working class. We were an earnest and moral generation, with severe politics. We were the last generation to defend communism. I knew people who holidayed in Albania; apparently the beaches are exquisite. An acquaintance supported the Soviet Union on the day they invaded Afghanistan.

We were dismissive and contemptuous of Thatcherism, but so captivated by our own ideological obsessions that we couldn't see its appeal. Which isn't to say we didn't fight it. There was the miners' strike, and the battles at Wapping. We were left enervated and confused. Soon we didn't know what we believed. Some remained on the left; others retreated into sexual politics; some became Thatcherites. We were the kind of people who held the Labour Party back.

Still, I never understood the elevation of greed as a political credo. Why would anyone want to base a political programme on bottomless dissatisfaction and the impossibility of happiness? Perhaps that was its appeal: the promise of luxury that in fact promoted endless work.

My friends and I talk of culture, the state of our

minds, and work. But rarely, now, of what could be; there are adjustments but not revolution. There have been enough revolutions. If Marx had been our begetter, the ideologue of the century's first half, Freud was our new father, as we turned inwards. Certainly, the world in which we negotiate our days at work, in love, in our hobbies, in sport – is one of other people, described, these days, in language derived from analysis. Most of my friends seem to spend most of their time on their backs, sleeping, fucking, or having therapy and talking about their 'relationships' on the phone.

The women, I think, were fortunate to go in two directions at once, into themselves and out into the history world. They examined their lives more than we did; they experimented; the interesting ones changed more than we did. What is left? The freedoms Nina takes for granted, a free girl swinging about the city. All is absorbed.

I never married Susan. She asked me several times, in a number of moods, hoping, I suppose, to move or amuse me with one or other of them. It might have been her liking for weddings that put me off, and her fondness for chiffon and those thick cardboard invitations with embossed writing. Certainly I enjoyed making her the only unmarried woman in her group of friends from university. She learned that her love involved sacrifice. Anyhow, I still took it for granted that not marrying was a necessary rebellion. The family seemed no more than a machine for the suppression and distortion of free individuals. We could make our own original and flexible arrangements.

I have been told the reasons for the institution of permanent marriage – its being a sacrament, an oath, a promise, all that. Or a profound and irrevocable commitment to the principle as much as to the person. But I can't quite remember the force and the detail of the argument. Does anyone?

Asif will know. He is an intellectual. But even he doesn't dangle his tongue in his wife's hole on principle.

I asked Nina to marry me.

'I can't,' she said.

'I won't ask again.'

'Yes, ask,' she said. 'Ask.'

Victor says marrying is too expensive. The women take all your money.

Not that Nina ever asked for anything. She was too

proud and scared of change for that. 'I don't want to be one of those well-fed women,' she'd say. 'Not yet,' I'd reply.

If I offered to give or lend her money, she looked horrified, as if everything, suddenly being made so easy, was devalued. Scarcity was part of her life, including love. Sometimes too much of everything is as bad as too little.

You pick up other people's feelings. Mother wanted to leave. She would stay; she would always have to stay. Women of her time had no money of their own and nowhere to go. They did, after all, have televisions and fridges. Inside she was on the run – from me; from all of us. Children stop you living. That's what her unhappiness told us. It's them or you.

Mother won't say much about my leaving. She is a little scared of me now, having angered me too much. But she will say that it is bad for the children. Odd how the needs of children seem so often to co-incide exactly with the opinions of their parents.

Not only does Susan work until seven, but she attends dinner parties, goes to the cinema and theatre, and sits on boards. She may be exhausted but she's involved. After I'm gone there will be devastation. A lone middle-aged woman with kids doesn't have much cachet, and Susan is always aware of her status. Successful and well-off, I was considered a catch, once. I was offered a lot of work, particularly from America. I wasn't precious about what I did; not precious enough, probably. But talent is always at a premium; everything else requires it. In certain moods she has been proud of me. A man can give a woman gravity and light. Perhaps she would rather have a busted, broken-backed relationship than nothing at all. At least there is someone to empty the dustbin. She will, unfortunately, become the recipient of sympathy. At dinner parties divorced men will be placed next to her. In the end, she will get by without me. In my view she'll be better off that way, though she can't see it yet. And I, without her?

Recently I have been tempted by a dream of self-sufficiency: a small flat, a cat, books, TV, music, a dope plant, friends to dinner; a museum on Sunday, followed by a bus ride to the end of the route with one of my sons. Alone but not lonely. I was living alone before I got back together with Susan. The first boy was conceived out of isolation, you could say, a few months after Father died. Yes; I understand the temptations of self-sufficiency, the idea that we can secure everything we need within, that our own caresses are as lovely as another's. But I don't want to be so seduced again. I will throw myself on others, going all the way, not hovering on the fringe of life.

Victor's flat is in a fashionable, bohemian part of town. There will be plenty of bars and restaurants to go to in the evenings. But he keeps most of his possessions in suitcases, and his washing in a pile in the corner with a damp towel on top. The only food in the kitchen is a loaf of bread, a rancid pat of butter, and several pots of jam, pilfered from hotels. To keep himself going Victor scoffs vitamin pills with his beer.

Victor has a disturbed mind, at times. His head booms like an ancient cavern filled with deadly creatures. I have considered it a sign of intense life to be so tormented. Victor yearns for quality of life, by which he means a quality of feeling, not things. But would you want to live with someone like that?

Three times a week he weeps at his therapist's. Five years and no sign of a cure. His therapist has told him to express himself. They offer such advice without considering the public. Who says self-expression improves your mental health? Look at the artists: art therapy every day. You'd think they'd be the sanest people around, Van Gogh, Rothko and all.

Victor gets competitive; men do. He wants what I have, and he wants to be like me. It's painful being him, but he asks for too much, and sometimes hates me for being myself.

I turn out the lights and find myself climbing the stairs to the bedroom. What am I doing? If this is my last night here, if these are, indeed, the final hours, hadn't I better get packed and ready? Soon I will be dead. Is it really the last night? No, no, no, never. Not really. I was only entertaining myself. Perhaps I will take a chance. That's a good idea. If she is awake . . . what? Yes; I will talk to her a little – after all, she has guided me out of confusion before. Then I will sleep, and continue as usual next morning. I will be glad to have endured this instructive and heavy discontent, but will have done nothing excessive.

I leave the light on in the hall. I step into the room.

I can make out your hair in the jumble of blankets and pillows. I stand looking at you.

I wish you were someone else.

Is it too much to want a tender and complete intimacy? Is it too much to want to sleep in someone's willing arms?

It's been weeks since we fucked. I've stopped approaching Susan in that way, to see whether, by any chance, she desires me. I have waited for a flicker of interest, not to mention lust or abandon. I am a dog under the table, hoping for a biscuit. Not a crumb.

Without removing my clothes I lie down. Yellow light streaks the room from the streetlamp opposite. It is a harsh, sickly colour, reminding me of the smell of gas. I look at the ceiling where the roof has been leaking. Someone has to be here to sort it out. Without me looking authoritative, the workmen could take advantage.

In the street there are raised voices. Most nights there is some kind of altercation. My neighbours punch one another, and worse, at every opportunity. Every couple of months a car is torched.

It's a mixed area: immaculate black women in

white smocks, head-scarves and long skirts go to the Farrakhan Centre nearby, the men in lounge suits and little red bow ties. Thin, efficient white boys in short-sleeved Ben Shermans, with short, neat hair, hurry to fights, carrying bags of chips. Black men in tattered shirts and shapeless trousers shamble to the pub on the corner. Smart women in black with brief-cases go to and from work. Outside the pubs wait women with pushchairs – the girl-babies with pierced ears – yelling through the open door at their permanently parked men staring up at the TV screen. The supermarkets have guards in ill-fitting uniforms watching you from the top of the aisle as you plump the fruit.

There's little to steal. There's more in my fridge than there is in most of the shops. You wonder why people put up with it. But they've got used to it; they can't see that things could be different. It is not how much that people demand which surprises me, but how little.

It is not a safe area, and in the morning I am going. Victor's wife, I remember, rang him urgently after he left, to say there had been an attempted burglary. He was surprised, on returning home, to see the windows had been broken – from the inside.

Now I am warm and getting dozy. The bed is comfortable. The house is silent; the children sheltered, healthy and asleep. She made a lovely meal. Having finished the wine, I have been contentedly swilling my brandy in the glass she bought me.

In India they don't seem to put the same emphasis on romantic love. Couples copulate when necessary and get on with their separate lives. In Lahore my uncle lives in one part of the house with his sons, three brothers, male friends, and anyone else who feels like staying a couple of years. My aunt, the daughters, female servants, and the children, live in another part. They meet, at times, but there is no funny business.

Perhaps it is a fine idea to have the women close but not too close. Presumably, over there they suppress their desire, but I am of a generation that believes in the necessity of satisfying oneself.

Maybe; but I have lost my relish for living. I am apathetic and most of the time want nothing, except to understand why there hasn't been more happiness here. Is it like this for everyone? Is this all you get? Is this the most there could be?

In the morning I will be gone.

It is my yearning for more life that has done this, and we are yearning creatures, a bag of insistent wants. Sense says one needn't follow every impulse, pursuing every woman one fancies. But one can, I guess, run after some of them, never knowing in advance what glory one might find.

Susan stirs.

Which scientist was it said bodies never meet? I stroke her back. I am convinced she can feel my thoughts, can feel me wanting her. If she wakes up, puts out her arms and says she loves me, I will sink back into the pillow and never leave. But she has never done such a thing; nor me to her. In fact, sensing my fingers on her, she moves away, pulling up the covers.

Why then don't I shake her awake and force her to look at me? Have I tried hard enough? Why should I imagine that I am easy to get along with? Perhaps, all this time, she has been making a heroic effort to get along with a morose, over-sensitive, self-absorbed fool. She said the other day, 'Imagine the strain of living with someone who doesn't speak for hours, and then says vaguely, "Have you ever thought of joining a cult?"' She has also complained about my scratching my arse almost continuously in bed so that it is a constant background noise, like the sound of crickets in a movie set in a hot place. There is no doubt that I have an aversion to shopping, housework, washing. Somehow I expect all that to be done without my having thought about it.

Nina, I remember, said I am inflexible. She called me a tyrant. Yes; my feelings are strong, my wishes imposing. Perhaps that is why I have had long periods, years in fact, of imposed indifference, as if nothing mattered. The dismissive shrug in a café was my most eloquent gesture. I was detached, having learned to be cold; intact, no one could touch me, particularly the women I let fall in love with me. I wanted them; I got them; I lost interest. I never rang back, or explained. Whenever I was with a woman, I considered leaving her. I didn't want what I wanted. I found their passion repellent, or it amused me. How foolish they were to let themselves feel so much!

Now I can hardly bear the strength of what I feel. Some nights I could bang my head on the wall, particularly when I've lain here with Susan, knowing that my girlfriend – whichever one, but usually Nina –

was out in the city. Perhaps she was missing me; probably she was with some young man. Aching at what I was excluded from, hating myself for my inability to live as I wanted, I have got up, dressed and left the house, walking a starlit misery until exhausted. I have returned to find that one of the kids has shit himself or vomited in his sleep.

Now, like Oliver Twist, I am asking for more.

In a few minutes I will wake her up and tell her some of these things.

How Nina tantalizes. She is aloof, feline, graceful. Everything she does has grace; some call it style. Others will say she knows who she is, and likes being herself. Her doubts don't undermine her, but they do make her inaccessible at times. I must be in love with her. I have yet to find out why.

So?

When did the realization really happen? When did it occur to me to leave? I can remember passing the critical point during one of my meandering conversations with Victor in the bar we go to. I thought, looking at all the free people ordering drinks, what's to stop me getting out and never coming back? But the idea was too cruel and subversive. Immediately I was filled with self-disgust, and saw myself from the back, running, a picture of all the other cowardly men who had fled.

That was eight or nine months ago. Nina and I would meet hurriedly before I had to be home with Susan. If there's nothing more likely to make you feel abandoned, desolate and left out than sexual betrayal, perhaps the only way not to feel it, is to feel nothing for the woman. It seemed a kind of freedom to encourage Nina to see other men, to have her tell me about them and for me to laugh at them.

'How many have you seen this week? And what did the last one do to you?'

'He kissed me.'

'And you let him?'

'Yes.'

'And then he puts his hands on you. And you, no doubt, put these hands that I'm kissing now on him. And –'

The more she told me, the more beautiful she looked. The more I removed myself, the more I hoped she would pursue me. Yes, I wanted her to follow me as I turned away, but I was also afraid of her feeling discouraged.

I have wavered, vacillated and searched myself for a reason to stay. But once the devil voice of temptation had spoken it wouldn't retract. Yet still I waited! For what? To be absolutely sure. 'Nothing's gonna change my world,' Lennon sang.

At home I made myself powerless and impotent. I could barely walk. What reason was there for putting one foot in front of the other? At night, when Susan was asleep, I couldn't turn on the lights; in the dark I wore sunglasses and hoped to fall over. Nina saw me shrivelling. If I was powerless I would be innocent. I couldn't damage anyone; blameless, I couldn't encourage retribution. I wished to be wishless!

For a year Nina visited me every two or three weeks at the flat I was using as an office. It was a roomy place, owned by an actor who was working in America. She was living in Brighton, where all runaways and lost individualists end up, teaching English to foreigners, always a last resort for the directionless. I met her – or picked her up; I was in that kind of mood one Sunday afternoon, feeling magnetic or 'on' – in a theatre café in London. It was a place I never normally visited, except that a photographer friend had an exhibition there. She was with another girl and as I looked at them I recalled Casanova's advice that it is easier to pick up two women at once than one on her own. After many smiles and a few words, I left. She came after me.

'Join me for tea,' I said.

'When?'

'How about in an hour?'

She stayed all evening. In a hurry for love after all this time, I behaved foolishly and, if I remember rightly, spent some time on my knees. She came back the next day.

She was a girl then, looking for someone to take the pressure off. She had run away from home when her mother's boyfriend smashed through the glass in the front door with his hands, and she was forced to hide in a cupboard. She was an unhappy and changeable girl, who often lost herself in inexplicable moods. She had never much been cared for, and kept herself apart. She needed to think she could get by without anyone.

When I first met her, she wore cheap, light, hippie clothes, and hadn't cut her hair. She still blushed and turned away her face. When she spoke it was in a voice so soft I could hardly make her out.

'What?'

'What is your situation?' she said.

'As regards what?'

'Everything.'

'Ah. My situation.'

'Yes. Will you tell me?'

'I will tell you.'

Unavailability can be so liberating. I asked to kiss her. She had to walk round the block to think about it. I waited by the window.

'Yes,' she said. 'Yes, I will.'

Soon we were exchanging the most intimate caresses while eschewing personal questions. In those days my favoured form of contact was the anonymous. Who could blame me for being afraid of the pulsation of feeling?

She said that I studied her constantly. She liked me looking at her.

I've never known a woman who wanted so much to be wanted, or a woman who was more afraid of it.

I've never known anyone make more arrivals and departures, not only on the same day, but within the same hour. I preferred her not to go out, and soon blamed her for having any life apart from me, which I considered an infidelity. This is what she shoved into her bag each time she left: hairgrips, slides and combs; little wooden boxes containing cheap Indian jewellery and hash; lip balm, nipple cream; tapes of the sound of the sea or perhaps of dolphins, birds or whales; camomile tea; a stuffed giraffe; postcards and photographs of cats; underwear, and other bits of the odd equipment necessary to mobile girls, as well as a certain amount of my wardrobe, including shirts, socks and my loafers.

Then, on her long legs, accompanied by a handful of good intentions and a head full of whims, she would make for the door as if pursued.

It made me fret about what it was out there she found so exciting – until I began to wonder about what it was in here that she found over-exciting. I learned that the more she loved me, the more she had to remind herself that she was separate. Understanding that nearly did me in as, from the window, I waved and watched her go. But at least I saw it.

I had just started to write a new film about an age-ing and fragile couple whose children have grown up and done well. The parents go to visit them, only to find their marriages are breaking up. I was excited by the idea and talked about it a lot so as to have her understand what I was trying to do every day.

She would lie on the floor beside my desk and watch me work. She said she envied my having something important to do every morning; something that absorbed everything; something to live for. My sense of purpose made her feel left out. She didn't believe I envied the fact that she woke up in the morning and wondered what she felt like doing that day. Would it be the dancing, pottery or a walk? She went to parties on the beach and in warehouses; she'd go any distance for a rave. She played guitar and sang in a group that I went to see. She dedicated all the songs to me. Not yet having acquired the glassy indifference of busy women in the city, she talked to people on the street and felt responsible for them. Her friends were dope heads in old clothes with woolly hats pulled down to their eyes. They were indolent and lacked the spark – like her and not like her. She drifted between boys. When she left them they suggested she considered herself too good for them. Too good for everyone but me.

I lay over her one afternoon. I had kicked off my slippers, and we had thrown the duvet down on the patio. She liked to make love outside, and I didn't mind, provided I didn't get a draught between my legs. The TV was on low. England were playing the West Indies. I was looking at her in awe and puzzlement, unable to understand how I could have such feelings for a girl I didn't know.

She used to say, 'You're so neat and gentle, with a soft voice. I've never met anyone who so much wanted the best for me. You know how to speak to people. You make them feel they can tell you the deepest things.' She seemed to trust me, as if she knew implicitly that she was safe, and that I would not let her down. But I did. In a strange way, she seemed to expect that, too. At least, then, she knew where she was.

There were mirrors in the bedroom we used. One afternoon, as I lay on the bed to wait for her, I caught a glimpse of myself. My body was thick and hairy, my stomach round, as if I'd swallowed a ball; my little prick stuck out merrily. I could have tied a pink

bow on it. In celebration of Wimbledon, I had prepared a handful of strawberries beside the bed, which
I intended to slot between her buttocks and guzzle
with cream. I watched myself lean over, pick up a bottle of cold champagne and press it against my balls,
before swigging from the bottle. She came into the
room in high heels, a suspender belt, my mac, and the
pearl earrings I'd bought her. I waved at myself in the
mirror! How happy I looked, as if all my epiphanies
had come at once!

I can't say I wasn't happy at that time. I liked to
compliment myself on having everything in balance.
I was also adapting a book for an American studio. I
knew they would have the script rewritten, just so
they would know they had been thorough. I was used
to that and reckoned they'd try a couple more writers
on it, before coming back to me. I had a tolerable partner and delightful children, as well as the perfect mis-
tress who, when she became pouty and sulky, I could
dismiss. I may have a hypocrite heart, but my vanity
was satisfied. As satisfactions go, that is ample.

One day she said, 'If you want me, here I am, you
can have me.'

'Thank you,' I said and added, some time later, not

wanting to take yes for answer, 'Do you mean it?'

She seemed surprised and reminded me that the third time I met her, when she enquired after 'my situation' I had said to her, 'You can do whatever you want with me. I am at your disposal.' And, apparently, I added, 'Don't think that I don't love you, because I do.'

I do.

Could I have done more with Susan? I mean, can I do more?

How little, when you think about it, can you will into being. Of what my parents and teachers tried to force on me as a child, little remains except a memory of abhorrence. I was never one of those kids who'd do things because they were compelled. All of me, along with the age, stood against compulsion. Such individualism has got me into trouble. You can, of course, will things for a while, but if you are alive you will rebel. You can protect and encourage the most delicate gifts – love, affection, creativity, sexual desire, inspiration – but you cannot requisition them. You cannot will love, but only ask why you have put it aside for the time being.

Susan and I cannot make one another happy. But the failure scars one, until it seems inevitable that such failure will attend all one's endeavours – if it is indeed happiness that one wants, rather than success, say, or sanctuary. My robust instinct, therefore, wasn't to give up but to persevere.

Susan had obviously been discussing our troubles with a friend. Therapy was recommended, as it always is to the minutely distressed. It saves friends the bother of attending to you. I refused to go. I imagined I needed my turmoil. I knew, too, that I didn't want to love Susan, but for some reason didn't want the clarity of that fact to devastate us both.

She made the appointment as briskly as always, giving the unexceptionable excuse that it was for the sake of the children.

I sat in the car feeling like a child being taken to the doctor by an impatient mother.

A few weeks before this, Susan and I visited a couple who had been married nearly a year. On the way I expounded my cheerful theory that people marry when they're at their most desperate, that the need for a certificate is a sure sign of an attenuated affection.

That night I noticed that the husband made a particular, loose-wristed gesture, using both hands when explaining something. I noticed this because it was obvious the wife detested the movement. She even said, while we were there, 'Can't you stop doing that?' In the car on the way home Susan and I laid bets on how long the marriage would last. We laughed for the first time in ages, and I wondered how much recognition there was in our mirth.

These days I think often of the couples I know or have met, and consider which of them is in love. There are some. It is tangible, you can see it between them, and feel the depth of their pleasure. Not long ago, at the kids' open day, I noticed a couple who were not engrossed in one another – they had things to do. But they were continuously aware of one another. Then, as their child ran about, and she thought no one was looking, she couldn't wait any longer, and she thrust her hand into her husband's hair and he kissed her.

No wonder everyone wants it – as if they have

known such love before and can barely remember it, yet are compelled ever after to seek it as the single thing worth living for. Without love, most of life remains concealed. Nothing is as fascinating as love, unfortunately.

I know love is dark work; you have to get your hands dirty. If you hold back, nothing interesting happens. At the same time, you have to find the right distance between people. Too close, and they overwhelm you; too far and they abandon you. How to hold them in the right relation?

It is beguiling how, in good relationships, even after years, formerly undiscovered parts of people are suddenly exposed, as in an archaeological dig. There is much to explore, and understand. With other people you can only turn away, bored.

I want to say: this is just the way things are.

I can't have been at my best the first time Susan and I visited the therapist. Once you know it is over there is no comfort in the present. Everybody was irritating me. I shoved strangers on the street. In the tube I pushed someone down the stairs, hoped to be arrested by the police and charged with possession of an uncontrolled mind. I rushed around the flat where I worked from one thing to another. My doctor, a friend, delighted in telling me about the range of available tranquillizers. But I refused to give him the pleasure of witnessing whether they provided tranquillity.

I was surprised we got to the therapist's at all without removing one another's windpipes with our fingernails. Susan and I passed the journey haranguing one another over the correct duration for the immersion of a teabag. According to her I had no facility for making tea, though I drank it all day, even – quite successfully – adding a little milk, on occasions, and sometimes a slice of lemon. But this was not good enough for Susan. I was hoping that the tea question would not come up with the therapist, at least not immediately: I am leaving because I cannot make her a cup of tea.

I could have poured hot water over her head, and Susan was ready to shove my testicles into boiling water, when we rammed the car into the therapist's drive and ran for her door.

I would imagine that therapy has benefited Victor. It gives him the opportunity to think of himself more than he always did, but less gloomily. He knows something of himself now. Whether he has changed is another matter. I suppose it depends on whether one sees self-knowledge as a benefit, and believes in it as the central purpose of mankind. Also, I have wondered whether there's a new class distinction emerging, between those who can afford to maintain their minds and emotions, cleansing themselves of toxic notions each week – and those who have to live with that which poisons them.

Yet despite my reluctance to go – to be coerced, once more – I had decided to confess all, to offer a few secrets without inhibition, such as they were. I wanted to be good at being helped. All the same, as we entered the room I stumbled, fancying I could hear the howls of pitiable couples trapped together for ever within the walls. I had to rest my face against the toilet wall and resist the idea of escaping through the window and absconding across the Vale of Health.

Susan and I sat side by side and six feet apart opposite a middle-aged and somewhat patronizing woman who had a 'concerned', if not pained, look. What a job, the harvesting of misery. She will never want for work.

Susan was soon into her second handkerchief.

The therapist, like me, appeared to sympathize with Susan, particularly when – in the attempt to get things started – I tried to define love as curiosity. I argued that unrest, disquiet, curiosity and the desire for more was at the root of life – you could see it in children. I said I had lost my curiosity about Susan. I said I had no passion to know her soul. She bores me; or I bore myself when I am with her. I said:

'All that matters is the hinge!'

The therapist leaned forward. 'What does the hinge mean to you?'

'The hinge?'

'Yes. How does it make you feel?'

I leaned towards her. 'The hinge of one's mind! Whether it opens inwards or outwards. Let it be outwards. Let it be – out!'

I fell back in the chair, ashamed of my desire, of all I wanted. That I couldn't want my life with Susan – which should have been enough – was inexplicable and cruel. The therapist, surely seeing the point of the hinge, would help me with this.

The woman, who presumably believed in the ungovernable desires of the unconscious, appeared, nonetheless, to be some kind of rationalist. She replied patiently that relationships did become less passionate. This was to be expected. Enthusiasm would be replaced by other consolations.

Consolations! Mad to learn what they were, I could have kissed those consolations from her lips!

'Yes?' I said.

'Contentment,' she murmured.

I leaned forward once more. 'Sorry?'

She repeated it: contentment.

She was all for maturity and acceptance. Yes!

Sobbing Susan was nodding.

How I wished I were nodding – with my face between Nina's legs, my hands holding her arse up like a dish I am hungry for, my tongue in all her holes at once – tears, dribble, cunt juice, strawberries! I suck the soup of your love. Soul doctor, therapist – who tickles their tongue in your old hole? I am not ready for the wisdom of misery; I have had that with Mother. I am all for passion, frivolity, childish pleasures! Yes, it is an adolescent cry. I want more. Of what? What have you got?

The therapist insisted we see her later that week.

Susan's fat, red weeping face in that room the second time, as I declare that I don't think things can be repaired. To have made it absolutely clear, I should have given her a back-hander or a finger in the eye. Then they would have understood! Instead, the therapist gets up and goes to the shelf where she extracts a book. She tries to get me to read a poem aloud. I glance over it. Seeing it is a bad poem, and being smart, I say I've forgotten my glasses. Ever-obedient Susan has to read it out in a tremulous voice, glancing at me in the old way, as if to say, later we will laugh at this. I keep thinking: I'm paying to hear poetry read aloud. I would pay not to hear this. Not even poetry can help us!

After my morning coffee Susan's blonde head coming through the open window of my flat in west London – a bunch of flowers, a book or a video behind her back. She wasn't working then, ten years ago. When I'd done enough for the day, she'd drive round in her little black car at the end of the morning, something tight around her breasts making them bulge and sway. I'd kiss her and pull her through the window.

We'd drive out to the country.

'Pull up your skirt,' I'd say, looking at her as we went, hoping for more. 'Higher!'

The morning after the first time, we went out for kippers and fried mushrooms. As we walked she put her arms around me. I remember, most of all, her grip. How she pulled me to her! If only I disliked her entirely, and weren't in love with Nina. What we like: English seaside towns, for instance, even in the winter. Certain jokes; her taste in food and pictures. Long discussions about English mod groups of the sixties.

There were other pleasures; there must have been. Or perhaps they were consolations. However, I cannot hunt for them now in the clutter of the past. Certainly, there are fewer of them than I might hope. Not a lot rushes to mind. I can't say that Susan has ever deliberately let me down or been more gratuitously cruel than necessary with someone as recalcitrant as me. I would give her a good reference.

'I have tried to make things work here!' she cried, yesterday. 'Every day I have wanted it to be nice for you!'

In front of her I am ashamed. But the truth is, I cannot amuse or arouse her. And yet, out of all the possible people in the world, we have chosen one another. For what? For a grave and difficult task: to frustrate and punish one another. But why?

I shove her a little, roughly, to see if she will wake up. She stirs, sighs, and sleeps on, oblivious.

How rarely are we really disillusioned! I am not leaving this unhappy Eden only because I dislike it, but because I want to become someone else. The dream, or nightmare, of the happy family, haunts us all; it is one of the few Utopian ideas we have, these days. And so I believe, despite everything – as I told Asif – in love. We begin in love and go to some trouble to remain in that condition for the rest of our lives. Isn't it the condition in which men and women are mostly likely to flourish? People become the most of themselves; sadists are sweeter, bankers more generous, coroners enjoy life, even bookmakers are sympathetic. And out there, tonight, in the shitty humming city, there is, I'm certain, someone to love me.

But then Victor believes that too. For three years he had an affair with a married woman he thought would leave her husband. She was, after all, unhappily married. But she preferred unhappiness to Victor. Was that failure? It ended; but perhaps the quality of a love can't be measured by its duration.

At university in the late sixties, Victor had been a radical. Now he lives in a decent flat and earns a good living. But there has always been one thing he has wanted. To have another chance at an ideal love, to marry the right woman, before it is too late for him to demonstrate his new-found enthusiasm, too late for him to play on the floor with his children – children who, this time, will not fling curses and his clothes out of the window after him. He wants to see if he can do it as it is meant to be done. That is all. The same as everyone else; not more, and not less. He needs to know that this most important of things is not beyond him. After all, a lot of people do it and some of them are happy.

Soon, therefore, there were others for Victor. Attractive women; good women. Some were a little zealous, particularly the American who, hardly having been into the bedroom, described to me how she intended to rebuild the flat. But none of them was right. Too old, too kind, too wrapped up in their career, too needy, too this, or too that. I'd meet a woman and think of him. We were all working on it, friends, relatives, even one of his children. Potential loves passed through his room like actresses auditioning for a part yet to be written.

He saw me with Nina, and he loved her. As long as she wasn't his, he could see what she was, and enjoy her. But as soon as the other stuff started with a woman – longing, missing, fearing, hoping – he was off. It was too much. Why can't he do it?

Why can't I?

Perhaps I can.

I don't want to wonder who Nina is with tonight as I lie here remembering how, when I came, she would hold my head and whisper in my ear, 'And I love you, and I love you . . .' She would caress my ears and compare them to those of the dog across the road when she was a child. I was flattered. It was a pointer.

I rub myself through my jeans. I wish I had someone to do this. Not everything can be achieved alone. I won't do it here. Susan is offended by my solo efforts. She is of a disapproving generation of women. She thinks she's a feminist but she's just bad-tempered.

Nina encouraged me to masturbate on her back, stomach or feet while she slept. She liked me to do it before she rushed off, to have me on her on the tube.

I want Nina but then I always want Nina when I have an erection. I will test my theory that one should masturbate before considering any woman seriously. That way one discovers if one wants her for sex, or whether there is anything more.

But this involves getting up. Increasingly I find myself adopting unnatural positions in order to move about at all. I have to sit down in order to put on my socks; my sons bring me my shoes, if they're in the mood. Then I have to tie my laces, straighten up, get to my feet, and move forward. Like my sons, when I am finally dressed, I consider it an accomplishment. Often, when I get into bed these days, all I do is remove my trousers. It occurs to me now that that could be the reason Susan finds me less attractive than she used to.

I raise myself quietly and tiptoe away from the sleeping woman.

How weak the arc of my urine is, and how I strain to send a respectable semicircle into the pan. Even when my boys were tiny, and those round little worms, their penises, were no thicker than a cable, the arc of their urine had a magnificent velocity. With me there is always a sticky mess on the floor. Dad had prostate cancer. They stuck metal and plastic instruments through the opening of his prick.

I have started to visit hospitals. I know where they all are now, without the *A-to-Z*. I think of my acquaintances: a woman I lived with for a week has got a brain tumour; another friend has throat cancer, and a good pal has had a stroke; cancer of the balls is rife. I am invited to more funerals than dinner parties. These are their bodies. I omit their minds for the time being. We are going down already, and before we have acclimatized.

On! Over the sink.

I push down my trousers and look for a suitable lubricant. The last time I did this, when Susan had some friends round for dinner, I used my children's shampoo, and felt as if a wasp had been pushed into my urethra. I should have complained to the manufacturer and had them conduct an experiment on animals. Even masturbation can be a medical minefield.

In the cupboard I find a greenish cream with a sugary smell. I stare at the label but find it difficult to make out the print without my reading glasses. After some examination I see that it is an anti-ageing unguent. God knows how much of our money Susan spends on this pig fat. Catching me once using it as hand cream, she became incensed. Maybe if I apply this every day to my prick it'll become fourteen again.

I stick my penis in it.

A few months ago I spotted someone I recognized in the corridor of a company I was visiting. Who is that, I thought, puzzled. Finally I recognized Susan, dressed in clothes too tight and modish, not to mention the purple nail varnish. She wasn't trying to look young, but hadn't realized how she had changed.

Lately, though, she has become concerned about the deterioration of her body. She said that after the second boy, she knew she would never get her previous face back. She could see herself now only in photographs. She always seems to be smoothing grease into the cracks in her face, and at the weekends she windmills in front of exercise videos, the boys and I sitting on the stairs. 'Mummy's getting thinner,' one of us will say optimistically. It isn't that she has become unattractive but that she has become middle-aged, and therefore of a different order of life. She receives, unfortunately for her, only serious consideration.

What if I met her now, for the first time, at a party? I would look at her twice, but not three times. It is likely that I would want to talk to her. Fearing those she can't seduce, she can be over-attentive to certain men, looking at them with what I call the 'enraptured gaze', until they wonder why she wants to appeal to their vanity rather than their intelligence. There are women who want to please men, and there are men who like to be pleased. You'd think they'd be enough for one another. But it is the women, I am convinced, who require this attention for themselves, and they soon resent the primacy they've given you.

I should have gone out with her for six months. Or maybe a one-night stand would have been sufficient. But I wasn't ruthless enough, and I didn't know what I wanted.

I begin to rub and pull my prick.

How long will she dislike me? A few months? Years? These partings or abandonments can cut deep. But disliking someone is exhausting; to hate them is to stifle oneself interminably.

Victor's wife still doesn't speak to him. She won't let him in the house but makes him sit outside in the car until the children are ready. It might have something to do with Victor persuading her to suck him off and swallow his come – something she would never previously do – the night before he left after fifteen years. By then he could only hate her. Ever since, she has sustained the loathing and bequeathed it to the children, as if her sanity depended on it.

Could I tolerate being disliked? Perhaps, somehow, we have an Arcadian fantasy that there will be a time when everyone will finally agree, that there will be no dissent, dissonance or strife. But one of the virtues of being a parent, I can see, is the ability not to mind being disliked by one's children. At times I hated Father. I would scream at him, even when he returned from the hospital after open-heart surgery. I put laxative in his cereal so he'd shit himself on the train. I hate my children, at times, as they must hate me. You don't stop loving someone just because you hate them.

Susan can be a virulent combatant, with a sharp tongue I've enjoyed. Unfortunately, her bitterness is too urgent to be witty; she lacks detachment. But her crude blows can hit the target. Nevertheless one soon tires of it. I am looking forward to the day when I won't give a damn what she says, when the spell will be broken.

What is it I require? A kind indifference, and some interesting underwear. As Scott Fitzgerald wrote, 'So we beat on . . .'

I sort through the laundry basket and extract a pair of her knickers, pulling them from her tights and laying them on the sink. Here we go. No; the grey knickers lack the *je-ne-sais-quoi*. Victor says I can become too self-depriving. The white might just do the trick. But perhaps the black with the lace trim have more dash. When it comes to self-abuse, I am an aesthete.

Is this an act of love or hate, or both?

I wish I had something to look at. Mind you, pinned to the wall is a postcard of the Matisse *Odalisque in Striped Pantaloons*. She is voluptuous, better than the best pornography. But life is the best pornography, I find.

Soon I am running through my library of stimulating scenes. Which one will I replay – the time in Berlin, or the middle-aged Italian who wept? What about the girl who rode her bicycle knickerless? Or perhaps the occasion I was wearing tight cowboy boots and adhesive trousers, and discovered, as the woman lay down for me, that I couldn't remove either my jeans or the boots, even with her pulling at them, and was forced to proceed with them on, in a kind of stumbling bondage.

In the old days it was possible scenes of the future – scenes that might actually occur – which I would use as an aid, rather than this nostalgia. And when, by mistake, I glance into the mirror and see a grey-haired, grimacing, mad-eyed, monkey-like figure with a fist in front of him, and the other hand placed delicately on his side because his back hurts from lifting the children, I know I am more likely to weep than ejaculate.

I was a child once, too.

I will think of Nina.

How often I am sitting in a bar or restaurant, or at a party with friends, and all I want is for her to walk in the door. I am under the impression that at that moment everything will be all right. No one else is as good as she is. There is so much I want to say. Our love is more important than everything else. Yet I am aware how susceptible to illusion we all are. How disturbing it is that our illusions are often our most important beliefs.

I don't think I can keep this up much longer. Before, the mere thought of a woman's body would have me spurting; now this act requires concentration and considerable labour. If there isn't some excitement soon, I'll get cramp or pull a muscle.

Three fingers, up to the knuckle, pushing inside you, stretching into the yielding flesh until it seems like a skin glove. 'It feels like a pulse,' you say. My hand is a part of you, yet it controls you.

Nina's face; then the way she turns over and offers her arse to me.

That should do it.

Christ. Yes.

I drop Susan's pants into the basket, reminded of D. H. Lawrence's remark that even animals feel sad after ejaculation. I wonder what observation could have led Lawrence to this knowledge. Still, I feel better, as if I wanted to rid myself of desire.

I am washing my hands when I hear a noise. Quickly I close my pants. The bathroom door is pushed open, as if by a ghost. I watch and listen.

From the darkness of the hall a child's luminous dummy bobs into the room, a tiny circle of green light. The boy's eyes are shut as he stands there in his Batman T-shirt, pyjama bottoms and furry slippers, three years old. Actually, he is asleep. He staggers suddenly, and automatically raises his arms as if he has scored a goal. My hands fit under his shoulders, I pull him up along my body, and smell and kiss his hair.

'What are you doing here, my beautiful boy?'

I carry him downstairs, put on a reading light and open the shutters. I lay him on the sofa and pull off his bottoms and soggy nappy. The smell is unpleasantly sharp and familiar at the same time; it is him. He is wilful and keeps trying to turn over, so I place one hand on the middle of his chest and push down, while grasping his ankles with the other as if I am about to hang him upside down from a hook. He thrashes and blinks as I wipe him. Then I shove and push to get the nappy in the right position. It is like trying to change the wheel of a moving car. I am terrified that he will start yelling. At last I replace his pyjama bottoms.

I hope he will do the same for me, one day.

Breathing hard, I sit at the window with him in my arms, whispering and blowing in his ear.

'Have I been good enough to you, little boy?'

I didn't enjoy him much as a baby, dreading the crying and whingeing, the refusal to get dressed, eat or go to sleep, as if my whole purpose was to get him to do things he didn't want to do. I was astonished how whole days would pass when there was no time for anything but him, not even in the evenings, and particularly not at night. Having considered several books on the upbringing of children, usually in the early hours, and often with faeces or vomit on my fingers, once I threw him backwards into his cot, hitting his head. I put brandy in his milk. I booted him hard up the nappy before he was even walking. How can children make us feel so helpless?

Susan cut me out too, keeping the babies and the competence to herself, her female friends and her mother. It has only been in the past few months that I've made myself useful. And only recently that I have fallen in love with him, which happened as it did with Nina, as an accumulation of amazement. His outlines became clearer and there seemed more and more to him, as door after door opened on wonder and pleasure, until I was captivated, cheered, moved. His smile; his laughter; his imitations of a cross face, of a funny face, of a sad face, delight me, as do his kindness and concern for me.

Now the boy and I talk ceaselessly. His questions – where does the light go at night, what do spiders eat, why do women have 'bosoms', where do people go when they die, and why do they have eyebrows? – are incessant. Where will he get the answers when I'm not here? If I tear myself from the boys, don't I tear them too?

When Victor left home his younger son threw Victor's belongings out of the window before sticking a broken bottle in his arm. He wouldn't have Victor visit him in the hospital. He wouldn't reply to Victor's letters. The other son lived alone in the family house when his mother went away. One night Victor found the boy lying on a sleeping bag in the hall, the only room in the house he used. All the lights in the house had blown or fused. He fed himself by candlelight, eating baked beans from the can. Old newspapers were piled up. The boy was unwashed, his clothes soiled. Surely Victor and his wife had taught the boy to clean himself? But, having had his world broken by his father's assault on happiness, the boy could barely speak or move. Victor is still repairing the damage.

I am leaving this woman alone with two young children. She will have to care for them, predominantly, herself. My presence, however baleful, has perhaps reassured her. Now she will work, buy their clothes, feed them, tend them when they are sick. I'm sure she will ask herself, if she hasn't already, what men are for. Do they serve any useful function these days? They impregnate the women. Later, they might occasionally send money over. What else could fathers be? It wasn't a question Dad had to ask himself. Being a father wasn't a question then. He was there to impose himself, to guide, exert discipline, and enjoy his children. We had to appreciate who he was, and see things as he did. If we grew up to be like him, only better qualified, we would be lucky. He was a good man. He didn't flee, though perhaps he considered it.

I pull the blanket from the back of the sofa and lay it across my son.

Sometimes the boy kicks and punches me, or rakes my face with his nails, and tries to bite me. He calls me 'a great big bully'. If I scold him, he sobs. If I become angry he stops himself breathing and can only gasp, as if I have taken his life. I feel guilty then, unable to bear the notion that the man he loves most has turned against him. We need one another, bully and boy. If I am away for a few days, travelling or idling somewhere, and I see children of my sons' age on the street or in a restaurant, I feel the panic of separation, and can't understand why I am not with my own sons. On my return I can see how they have changed. I don't want to miss a moment of them. Not only for the sake of their future, but for now, this moment, which is all there is.

It is always them I think of before I fall asleep. And I am leaving.

Yet the children are more agitated than usual when Susan and I are together with them, as if our furies are infectious and they are weeping on our behalf. Perhaps if we continued to live together they would dream of running away. Susan wanted to send the younger boy to 'see someone'. I said, when the parents go mad, they send their children to psychiatrists.

'It's you who has gone mad,' she said. 'Your theories are insane.'

Cheerio, bitch.

But there is something else I have to face.

When I leave I want her to vanish too. There may be little love, but jealousy remains. I want to live my life but don't want her to live hers. When this is done – and eighteen months, say, have passed, as they surely will – there may be another man in this house. He might be sitting where I am now. My sons, if they have a nightmare, will go to him. Children, who have yet to learn our ways, are notoriously promiscuous in their affection. They'll sit on anyone's knee.

The man will kiss and hold them when they wake up. He might put them to bed and talk to them until they sleep. He might have a northern accent. He might encourage them to support Arsenal. Or perhaps he will become impatient and flick the back of their heads By then I could be an outsider, sitting in the car waiting for them to come out of the house. And the boy won't remember this night. Neither of them will remember their parents together. They will remember none of this and I will never forget it. She will always know them better than than I will.

Still, I hope she ends up with someone rich. Not that there will be a queue, I hope. Nevertheless, the most grotesque people get laid, and even married. As Joe Orton says, 'Marriage excludes no one the freaks roll-call.'

The therapist kept saying, you are leaving the children too, don't fool yourself about that. I wanted to shout, no, no, it's her! But we had the children together, which was an assumption of trust and security, that I will break.

At times I feel sorry for the children, having to stay here with her. I can clear out, but they can't.

The boy is sleeping soundly. I love hearing his dreams, and discussing them with him. Susan sneers at my pretentiousness.

I should sleep now. But I would rather not go to bed. There are few things more desolate than undressing in the dark beside a woman who won't wake up for you.

Often, at the thought of going home, blood will rise into my head, pressing into my ears and eyes, until I feel my skull is bulging like an overinflated tyre. I might go to some filthy bar and hold on to a chair, or to someone's house where I could get a grip on the host's wife. One night I arrived late at a dinner party. As usual the women were talking about work and the men about children. I took my place and saw nothing for it but to drink. Things looked up when a middle-aged acquaintance laid his finely coiffured head on the table. His wife, whom he'd left, was refusing to let him see their children, and was, he believed, turning them against him. She was also refusing to sell the house in which his money was tied up. They were going to court. And the acquaintance, with his new young girlfriend at his side, was saying he doubted whether it had been worth it.

The girlfriend replied that he had let the children wreck their romance. It was him she wanted, not the children he'd had with a woman he didn't love. Around the table, other sombre men whose last glimpse of their wives had been at the door of the divorce court, nodded, grumbled and shook their heads. Then the woman got up and left. I should have run after her. My wet-eyed acquaintance said he had given up most of what he had had for her. But when, after a couple of months, they realized that they didn't much like one another, and, in fact, she had tried to tear one of his ears off, there was no way back – no way back to anything solid.

All that for a fuck, I muttered. The other men

laughed. But I concluded, having just seen how the little minx fondled the house cat as her lover wept, what a fuck it must have been. A discussion followed, around the table, on the ethics of such a dilemma. But I could only think that there are some fucks for which a person would have their partner and children drown in a freezing sea. My kingdom for a come. Women, I've noticed, are particularly tenacious in this respect. When they want someone there's no stopping them.

My son, there may be a time when I will explain some of these things to you, because there may be a time when I understand them.

Holding the back of his head with one hand, and supporting his back with the other – his eyes are closed and his mouth open – I carry him to bed. But as I am about to lay him down I have a strange feeling. Sometimes you look into a mirror and can't always remember what age you are. Somehow you expect to see a twelve-year-old, or an eighteen-year-old, looking back at you. Now I feel as if I am looking at myself. He is me; I am him; both of us part of one another, but separate in the world. For now it is myself I am carrying in my arms.

I lay him down and cover him up.

I wonder when I will sleep beside him again, if ever. He has a vicious kick and a tendency, at unexpected moments, to vomit in my hair. But he can pat and stroke my face like a lover. His affectionate words and little voice are God's breath to me.

I creep down the stairs. I put my jacket on. I find my keys. I get to the door and open it. I step out of the house. It is dark and cold. The fresh wind sweeps through me. It invigorates me.

Go. You must go.

I am kicking over the traces.

You could go into the dark and fear that you will never emerge.

This must be the death hour, the lowest part of the night. Barely a living thing is moving, including me.

Outside, the dark leaves on the trees flap in the wind like hundreds of long green tongues, the branches knocking at me.

I will roll a joint, if I can. This grass smells obnoxious. Like a damp bonfire, Susan says, particularly if I smoke it without tobacco.

I like watching the plants grow at the back of the

garden. When I get home in the evening after a few drinks, and there is nothing for it but to shut the front door, and I know I have to remain under this roof until the morning, as if I am under some kind of house arrest, one of the few things I do like is to go out into the garden. There I spray away at my dope plants, with my youngest boy, packed into his Babygro and felt shoes, tugging and pulling at the hose pipe behind me.

Occasionally I strip off a few leaves, wrap them in newspaper and dry them on the boiler. I have Ecstasy, LSD and an old bottle of amyl nitrate in the fridge. For a while I'd take the 'E' every day, starting after breakfast. It made me feel worse, and I knew it. But I didn't stop. I have always preferred to take drugs in the straightest situations, at supper with my parents, for instance. I still do the occasional parent–teacher evening, in my latest favourite suit, on acid. The annual nativity, I find, is always improved by a tab of Purple Haze. It is the secrecy I enjoy, and perhaps the challenge.

Nina used to tease me, saying my attitude towards drugs belonged in another era. It is true that when I was growing up, drugs were fuel for a journey into the self. They also connected me with a more danger-ous and defiant world, and even a literary one: De Quincey, Baudelaire, Huxley. For Nina they mean sordidness, prison, and overdoses. It was her fear of needles that had kept her safe, if she is safe.

I've decided to forget the pinstripe suit. It'll get crumpled in my bag and there's nowhere to hang it over there. The Lennon picture is a definite. But I must find a photograph of the children to take with me.

I go to Susan's desk, which is covered in her papers. Hoping to find evidence of some recent betrayal for which I can reproach her and then walk out, I snatch up her wallet and open it. I find only a picture of us with our arms around one another.

In the drawers there are packets of photographs. I select one of my eldest boy a few days old. I am bathing him in the hospital, his head lying in my hand. My face is grave with concentration as I splash his ribs and screwed-up face for the first time. It was Karen I was seeing then. I waved goodbye to Susan in the hospital, picked up the champagne her father had left us, and drank it in bed with Karen. Susan men-tioned it the other day.

'I will never forget that you left the hospital without kissing me. Our first child, and you didn't kiss me. Still, at least you love the children. When you go away.'

'Go away?'

'Travel. The children ask for you all the time. The first thing they say in the morning is, "Is Daddy coming home today?"'

I put the photograph in my pocket.

For old times' sake I glance through her journal. It's dusty; she doesn't keep it regularly, but only writes down the things she wants me to read. I glance over the passage in which she wrote, three years ago, of her lover, wondering if she should visit him in Rome. I could see through her lies and told her I would be glad if she went. I was always looking for opportunities to leave her.

I return to my position on the sofa. I will smoke more of this, though it makes me feel I have been handed over for public accusation.

'There you are.'

I look up. I look away. I look back again. Susan is at the bottom of the stairs in her white T-shirt and white slippers, her face creased and puffy.

She looks so white I could write on her.

Once, coming home at four, having walked back from some teenage party, I found Mother downstairs in her floor-length stained dressing gown. Scattered on the floor were photographs of her as a young woman. In those old prints she was gawky and keen, with hair as long as mine, sandals, and a flowered dress. She was posed with men who had partings and ties, none of them Father.

Susan must have been watching me staring into space. For how long, I wonder?

I liked taking Nina to restaurants and parties, to openings and exhibitions. I would sit and watch her looking at the pictures. I took pleasure in her pleasure as I led her around London. I wouldn't have gone out otherwise. Our hands were always on one another. Wherever we were, she was my refuge, my pocket of light. But these new pleasures extracted her from a familiar world and pushed her into an intimidating one. I overwhelmed her at times. There was too much of me, I know that. We want love but we don't want to lose ourselves.

Asif was marking papers, surrounded by his alpha-
betically arranged books on philosophy, education
and child development. On his desk were pictures of
his wife and children. When he saw me this afternoon
at his study door, with Najma standing concernedly
behind me, he was alarmed. Perhaps I looked
strained, or worse.

'The children are well?' was the first thing he
asked.

'Yes, yes.'

He was relieved.

We shook hands then.

'And yours?' I say.

'Thank God, yes.'

Najma said with a challenge in her eyes, 'And
Susan?'

'Fine. She's fine.'

Asif looked at me enquiringly. I didn't like disturbing his peace. I didn't even know why I had come. I
had been walking the streets since morning. Then I
hailed a cab and told the driver Asif's address. Perhaps because Victor is a recent convert to hedonism I
required the other view.

I said, 'Can I speak to you?'

Najma left us reluctantly and Asif exchanged his slippers for his outdoor shoes. I realised that he is getting fuller, and with his waistcoat pulled tight across his stomach, he looks older, more dignified and substantial.

We walked in his garden. I noticed he kept looking up towards the conservatory where Najma was reading in a wicker chair. I fancied she was already condemning me.

I said, 'The house is full of poison. Susan wants me to be kind. I can't be kind. We can do nothing for one another. It is a fact. I have decided to leave.'

Asif said, 'All couples fall out. Even Najma and – '

I said, laughing suddenly, 'But I remember.'

'What?'

'Over the omelettes at breakfast. Before we went down to the pool – on holiday in Italy last year. Susan and I were civil to one another for hours at a stretch. But you two. The silences. The resentment. You couldn't wait to get to that café where you and I could play table football alone.'

'Fair enough. She and I disagree . . . at times.' Then he said, 'It is easy to turn away too soon. Why be hasty? See what happens. I beg you to wait a year.'

'I can't wait another week. In fact I am off in the morning.'

'Surely not? But a year is nothing at our age. Is it because of the girl?'

I shrugged. 'I don't see her. I've lost her.'

'Don't – you are shivering.' He put his arm around me. He said, 'But you are following her in some way?'

'If I could see the hair on her neck again, I could move outwards from that point. That would be the start, you see, of a new attitude.'

'Her hair?'

'Of course.'

'It's only that I didn't realize men of our age could get so romantic.'

I said, 'Asif, no age is excluded from strong feeling.'

He snorted. 'What a pity you ever met her!'

'Why do you insist on finding this risible?'

'Perhaps I hate to see a man I respect, who is brave and dedicated in some ways – and stubborn in others – blown about by such passions. But I suppose, unlike most people, you can afford to follow your pleasures. And follow them you do.'

'Yes. But don't think I don't know that there are

more important things to think about – the international political situation, and all.'

My sarcasm silences him.

His children run about. They ask for my boys. I say they are at home. Other children's voices rise up from nearby gardens. Kids come to the side gate.

If only I could sit here contentedly in the middle of my life as children seem to in theirs, without constantly worrying about the state of things, tomorrow, next week, next year. But since the age of fourteen, when I conspired against my parents, not fleeing as I intended to, but biding my time and preparing, knowing one day I would be ready, I have required the future as a goal. I've needed something to happen every day that showed a kind of progress or accumulation. I can't bear it when things go slack, when there isn't sufficient intensity. But I would welcome a quiet period. I am hoping for that, in the long run.

He said, 'You're very distracted. I know you like to look after yourself, but you haven't even shaved. Leaving aside your girlfriend's hair for a moment, your own looks as if you've been combing it vertically.'

I laugh but say nothing.

After a time he says, 'You've made up your mind?'

'I think so.'

'I don't want you going to some dismal bedsit. Come here if you want, for a while. I'll put the children in together.'

'You are kind, Asif. Thank you. But I couldn't sit here in the middle of your family life after leaving my own.'

'It won't be for long.'

'Sorry?'

'After a few days' reflection, you'll decide to go back. You are not prepared to miss the children. I don't think you quite realize what it will feel like . . . to leave them. It will hurt them, won't it?'

At that moment my legs almost gave way.

I said, 'I know I will have to go through that.'

He said, 'The new girl you called one of the uneducated educated. Susan is spiky but she is intelligent. I've always enjoyed talking to her. You must, once, have had good reason for choosing her.'

'Aren't I allowed to change my mind? If people are rushing away from one another in droves, it is because they are running towards other people.'

'All of us yearn for more. We are never satisfied. Wisdom is to know the value of what we have. Every day, if there is some little good fortune, and our children smile at us or for once do what we say, we should consider ourselves lucky.'

'I am discouraged. An unhappy relationship can't be a sealed compartment. It seeps into everything else, like a punctured oil can.' I looked at him. 'You've never considered throwing it all away?'

We both glanced up towards Najma.

'Why do you ask me this?' he said exasperatedly. 'Do you think, one day, that I will give a different answer and your view of things will be confirmed?'

'Asif, what view of things?'

'That one doesn't have responsibilities.' He sighed and went on, 'I'm sorry. I suppose what you are doing is the modern way.'

'I would say that there is a new restlessness about.'

'Yes, it makes me feel unique for loving the same person continuously for a number of years and not covertly planning an escape. But I do love it here. Every day something is built upon. There is increase. Without it I would be just a man walking down the street with nowhere to go.'

'At home, for me, there is no movement.'

'With a real love there is little movement. You are going round and round, but further and further. Don't you believe in anything? Or is virtue only a last resort for you?'

What could I say here? Young people are full of tedious belief. Why not me? Not many beliefs come spontaneously to mind. We have reached such a state that after two thousand years of Christian civilization, if I meet anyone religious – and, thankfully, I do only rarely these days – I consider them to be mentally defective and probably in need of therapy.

I might say: I believe in individualism, in sensualism, and in creative idleness. I like the human imagination: its delicacy, its brutal aggressive energy, its profundity, its power to transform the material world into art. I like what men and women make. I prefer this to everything else on earth, apart from love and women's bodies, which are at the centre of everything worth living for.

But Asif is intelligent. I don't want to embarrass myself by saying anything too selfish – though I can think of few more selfish institutions than the family. Perhaps I am becoming a committed sceptic.

Probably I am giggling now. I'll speak before he considers me mad.

'I have my opinions,' I say. 'But they're unimportant. They change every day. It's always something of a relief not to have an opinion, particularly on cultural or political questions. But I tell you, when it comes to this matter, it is an excess of belief that I suffer from.'

'Belief in what?'

'In the possibilities of intimacy. In love.'

He almost laughed. Then he said, 'You've always liked women. You haven't grown out of it.'

'But they are likeable. Haven't you noticed?'

'What about someone on the side?'

'You're suggesting that?'

'You travel a lot. You're always in America, turning literature into –'

'Pap.'

'There must be opportunities. It might take away the need.'

'It does, for a time. But it depends entirely on precisely what the need is and whether it can be taken care of. Or whether it renews itself, and with how much ferocity. Anyhow, you wouldn't do it.'

He said, 'Don't forget I am a teacher.'

'I know. Why are you saying this?'

'Teaching is difficult, you know. And it is made even more difficult if the children are distressed. In the classroom I see the debris. The fall-out. The broken side of things.'

He offered me tea.

I couldn't stay any longer. It was time to get home, bathe my children, see Susan, and pack. I had to make my contribution to the broken side of things.

Victor says, 'It was the worst, and also the best thing I have done. For two years after I left I was aware at the back of my mind that something unforgivable had happened. I knew that not far away, people – my wife and children – were suffering as a result of what I had done. However – '

He continues, 'You might mock me for the saveloy and chips, and the juicy pickled onion in particular. But how many of our friends and acquaintances, having left their partners, would wish to go back to them? How many of them would say, were they able to relive that period, that they wouldn't have left?'

*

'What's the matter? Are they sick? Are they awake?'

'No,' she says.

Susan looks both.

She comes to me from the bottom of the stairs, arms outstretched.

'Hold me. Not like that, as if your arms are tongs. Touch me with your hands.'

I remember my eldest son saying, 'Why do we have hands?'

I say, 'I'm here now.'

'Yes. Thank God. Hold me.'

I kiss her and move my hands over her. Her T-shirt rides up. Inadvertently, I touch her breast. I reach down. Her pubic hair is not as luxuriant and soft as Nina's. But if she lets me fuck her here, now, on the floor, I won't leave. I will put my straight shoulder to the wheel and accept my responsibilities for another year. Anyhow, in the morning I'll be too tired. I will get a kipper out of the freezer, scoff a big breakfast and breathe a sigh of relief. I like a happy ending.

She says, 'I had a bad dream – that you weren't here. Then I woke up and you weren't there. You're not going to leave, are you?'

'What makes you say that?'

'I don't know, I don't know.'

'It's okay,' I say. 'Calm down, I'll massage you.'

'No, thank you. You don't know how to do it. You are too rough.'

'I see.' I say, 'It's not as if you ever touch me.'

'Are you surprised?' She says quietly, 'You're not, are you?'

Lying I don't recommend. Except in certain circumstances.

Susan, if you knew me you would spit in my face. I have lied to you and betrayed you every day. But if I hadn't enjoyed those women I wouldn't have stayed so long. Lying protects all of us; it keeps the important going. It is a kindness to lie. If I'd been good all those years, who'd have been impressed? God? A world without lying would be impossible; a world in which lying wasn't deprecated is also impossible. Unfortunately, lying makes us feel omnipotent. It creates a terrible loneliness. Here, tonight, I feel cut off from you and from everyone. Truth telling, therefore, has to be an ultimate value, until it clashes with another ultimate value, pleasure, at which point, to state the obvious, there is conflict.

She begins to wake up.

'What are you doing down here? Why aren't you in bed?'

'I had things to do.'

'At this time?'

'I couldn't sleep.'

'Why? What's bothering you? Usually you're barely awake.' Her eyes sweep my face. 'You smell of cigarettes and that awful dope. Your hair's wet. Did you go out? Where did you go? Who did you see?'

Her fingers are on my cheek.

'Ouch.'

'What is that? What's happened to your face? Wait – '

She goes to the light switch and, as she moves, so sleepy is she that she stumbles and falls against the table.

Let me catch you.

Tonight the streets smell of urine. Lorries are parked outside the supermarkets; men push metal containers through the side doors. Young people are out, going somewhere.

Seven years ago, when Susan and I separated for a

year and I could be excited by strangers, I knew these bars, knew girls who sold jewellery in the market, people in bands, travelling kids. I had time for the unexpected.

Tonight, having changed the boy's nappy, returned him to his bed and driven to this bar without knowing why, all I see are dozens of ageing young people in improbable and cheap clothes, pressed together. I know no one. My current friends I meet only by arrangement, making appointments with them as one would with a dentist. And Victor, five years older than me, was never going to be in such a place, though, to his credit, he has taken up dancing. He goes to clubs, sometimes alone, where he starts a peculiar, independent, Terpsichorean movement. Soon a space opens up around him. I'm not sure if this is because of his individual style or because people think he's an AWOL policeman.

'I don't mind being a fool,' he says. 'But stylish young people can be very snobbish.'

Outside the bar there are dudes in knee-length thick coats, baggy trousers and boat-like trainers. Funny how drug dealers always stand around doing nothing for ages, before suddenly walking quickly. Tonight I wonder if they have all, simultaneously, been afflicted with head pain, as they clutch their skulls as if posing for Munch's *The Scream*, while speaking into mobile phones. Once, I would have asked the price of this or that drug. Now I consider what will happen to them, and wonder why they have wasted their money on such clothes. But then they would think that I lacked distinction.

I did see someone I knew in the bar. A kid no longer a kid who, at one time, I had seen every day for a few weeks. In my socialist phase I would listen to the misfortunes of such a boy at length, and condemn the society that had made him suffer. He had been lively and smart and full of stories about his adventures on the street, but injured within, making his bravado more poignant. In the bar he stood up against me, wheedling and demanding a thousand pounds to go and live on an Indian Reservation.

I listened to him before saying, 'You'd think they'd have enough problems without you.'

I try to push past him but he holds on to my hand.

'You can afford to help another human being,' he

goes, putting on his most pathetic look. 'Out of the kindness of your – '

I interrupt him, 'I'll give you the money if you tell me this one thing. Where is your father? Why aren't you at home with him?'

He looks at me.

I say, 'Answer me!'

'What have you been taking?'

He wheels away.

Out on the street I could easily start gesticulating and yelling, for I believe some of these men don't know their fathers. Where have all the fathers gone? Once the fathers went to war and returned, if they did return, unrecognizable. Yet still the fathers flee and return, if they return at all, unrecognizable. Do they think about their children? What better things do they have to do? Is it when their women become mothers that they flee? What is it about the mothers that makes it so essential that they be left? Where are the fathers hiding and what are they doing?

Someone must know. I must ask one of them. I must ask myself.

I run to my car. Tonight there is one other place I must visit.

Victor was always kissing Nina and putting his arm around her. He patronized her but, seeing how awkward he is, she took care not to scare him.

One night at his place Victor had some new drugs. When he had become lost in some unknown place, Nina and I started to make love. Victor got into bed with us. How I regret what I wanted to do – which was reduce her in my mind. If she weren't special, my feeling for her wouldn't be as strong.

'Why did you do it?' I asked him.

'You were laughing. You were enjoying yourselves.'

I did know how to please her. I would cook for her; I would bathe and massage her while she listened to music. I swore I could love, protect and support her.

She trusted me but was becoming discouraged.

She told Victor, 'He keeps leaving me. Every time I get used to him again, he goes home, or worse, on holiday. I am losing hope. I feel suffocated. I don't even know what I am waiting for.'

She told me she couldn't see me for a while. She needed to distance herself. I had Victor keep an eye on her, ring her every day and keep me alive in her thoughts. One day, in a truculent and spiteful mood, I asked him if he would go out with her if I weren't around.

I think they saw each other for a couple of weeks. I didn't enquire, and I didn't talk to him as I was away with Susan and the children. Then he rang and told me that she'd asked him not to get in touch any more. He and I resumed our friendship. We didn't speak about Nina. I thought I would soon forget her.

'I went to a bar for a drink. It was crowded. I decided to have a stroll. Then I saw a club and went in and walked about.'

'You just saw a club.'

I say, 'Yes, a line of people on the street.'

'What made you go in?'

'I don't know. I think it was the kind of thing I would have enjoyed, before.'

Susan says, 'It's not like you to be spontaneous. Where is your shirt? Weren't you wearing a shirt earlier?'

'God, yes, I was,' I say. 'How easy it is to lose things!'

She stares at me.

*

Having not found Victor in the bar, and the streets seeming more violent than I remember them, I drive to the house where she had a room. I went there several times a few months ago, when she moved to London, to be near me, as she admitted. Her fantasy, she said, was of living around the corner.

The kitchen was always crowded with young people either recovering from some dissipation or preparing for it. I remember her bed on the floor; an Indian coverlet; poetry books; tapes, and the numerous candles that make Christmas so exciting for young women.

'I don't know why I'm living here,' she said, as I dragged myself away from one bed in order to return to another. 'I should be with you. Can't you stay for ever, or at least tonight?'

I looked at her, naked on the bed, as white as a grain of rice.

'How I wish I could.'

'You see, I don't think I can bear this for much longer.'

'Won't you wait for me?'

'I don't know.'

Tonight I loiter outside, though there is nothing to

see through the window. At last I ring the bell. A young man comes to the door. I ask him if he remembers me. He does, though with so little enthusiasm that I wonder if he was one of the people who advised Nina against me.

'Does she still live here?'

He looks at me suspiciously.

He says, 'She was away for a time.'

'She was?'

'She came back.'

'She did? She came back? Could I see her? Is she in?'

'No.'

I refrain from slapping him.

At last he informs me that he thinks she has gone to a club nearby.

'Who with?' I say.

'A friend.'

'Where is it?'

Sighing, he tells me, as if I should know such things.

I drive down there and stand in line for an hour, terrified they are not going to let me in. As I near the doormen, I remove my shirt in the hope that this will make me seem more contemporary. I conceal it behind a hedge across the road, so I am wearing a T-shirt and jacket.

Inside it is like a disco, only dark, practically black, without the flashing lights that so entertained me as a teenager.

One problem: if she were here I wouldn't be able to see her.

For most of my life, until tonight, I have been young. For most of my life, there were people to look up to, who seemed to know what was going on. Where are they? These days, apart from when I am with Susan, I know who I am. When necessary I can gather myself together and maintain some dignity. But tonight I'm losing it.

Igniting my lighter, I push through the crowd, as if I am exploring a cave.

People are wearing outdoor coats buttoned up to the throat, with pulled-down hats. There's no doubt, British kids are innate meritocrats, and satirists. You can be sure they're always up to something. But tonight it is depressing to see young people so drugged and stupefied. I want to ask why, as if I can't remember. Three years ago, for six months I took cocaine all night every day. It was luck and ambition that kept me clean in the end. Were we such undemanding zombies, and did we believe that being young was a virtue in itself? Undoubtedly. Do my taxes subsidize their indulgence? Probably. Did my father walk uncomprehendingly about such places looking for a young woman to hurl himself at?

I fear for my sons, but it is essential that I leave them tomorrow.

I think I have become the adults in *The Catcher in the Rye*.

Why do I envy these people? In the late sixties and seventies I did feel that I belonged to something, to other young people, and to some sort of oppositional movement. The earnestness I disliked; I was too awkward to join things. But there is something I miss: losing oneself, yes, in a larger cause.

As I press my lighter into the faces I begin to dread the thought of seeing her. What if she is with a young man? What if she despises me now? These faces are young. I must have been insane to fall for such a part-woman. What is wrong with maturity? Think of the conversations I could have – about literature and bitterness – with a forty-year-old! Victor has mentioned an interesting optician with her own shop. People say it is the soul not the body that counts!

I know a place where I could meet some middle-aged women, if they are up so late! Once I level out they will be grateful for my company! They are a larger cause!

I will seek some out!

I begin to make for the door, wherever it is, with some urgency. This is typical of me – to be so close to something, and then flee.

I catch sight of a woman dancing on her own. Surely it is her? I move towards her. No; it is not my love. I can't make out much, but get the impression this woman won't mind if I approach her. Apparently the drugs they take make them friendly, as if they could not manage it otherwise. Perhaps they should give them to all young people. Surely, in such a mood, they won't care if you dance like a crashing helicopter? I want to learn to expect to be received kindly by people.

I shout in the woman's ear and she comes with me to the bar. I can't hear much of what she says. But I imagine going home with her. If she says yes, I will go. A strange room; her things; odd places I have ended up in the past, lost in the city, waiting to see what will turn up. From there, in the morning, I will leave for Victor's without going home.

I was hit then. It seemed to be from behind, and it was a man. It might have been when I examined the ring through the woman's eyebrow by the flame of my lighter. She would have interested Victor.

Susan sits down beside me.

'Don't touch it, it's only where I got punched,' I say.

'Were you aggressive?'

'Why it happened, I don't know. It is just what young people like to do. It'll be okay by tomorrow.'

'What is this?' she asks.

'A signed photograph of John Lennon.'

'Why was it on the stairs?'

I look at her in puzzlement. 'Was it? I think I was looking for a better place to hang it.'

'In the middle of the night?'

'It seemed to be the right time.'

'It's cracked now,' she says. 'Look at the glass.' She says, 'Your poor face. Do you want me to bathe you?'

I look at her and say, 'There is someone I'm interested in. But she's gone away. That's the truth, I'm afraid.'

'You? There's someone interested in you?'

'It surprises you?'

'Well, yes.'

'I am surprised that you are surprised.'

She is crying.

'Is she going to take you away from me?'

'I shouldn't think so, now.'

I open my mouth. I am about to speak.

'What is it?' she says.

'No. Nothing,' I say. 'Come along.'

In the bathroom she bathes me. Then I lead her back to bed, my hand on her arm.

We lie there, back to back.

What could be more dreadful than daylight? She is dressing at the end of the bed. The children are bouncing on the mattress. The younger one tries to open my eyelids with his fingers. The other pours apple juice in my ear, wondering whether it will exit through the other. He has the makings of a scientist.

Susan goes downstairs with them.

I turn on to my back, as I do every morning, and think, what do I have to do today? What obligations do I have? What pleasures might there be? Then I remember and shut my eyes.

After a time the front door bangs and the house goes silent. The silence increases, enveloping everything in an ominous softness.

I get up and go down the stairs, but a noise makes me hesitate at the bend. I can see that in the hall Susan is leaving for work, putting her short coat on and pushing her bicycle to the door.

'Will you get something for later? See you at supper time!' she calls out, shutting the door behind her.

Without eating, drinking or thinking excessively, I do everything as quickly as I can. I shave and get some decent clothes on. Moving about the house, I discover my boys' night clothes flung on the floor. I pick them up, smell them, and fold them on their beds.

When the weather is warm, Susan puts talcum powder in her shoes and when she removes them her footprints remain on the floor, traces of her on the carpet, which stop suddenly, like a trail gone cold.

Soon I am zipping up my bag.

Standing up, I scribble a note. 'Dear Susan, I have left this house and won't be coming back. I'm sorry to say that I don't think we can make one another happy. I will speak to you tomorrow.' That is it. Then I notice she has left a note asking me to pick up her dry cleaning. Cursing, I hurry round the corner to fetch her clothes, and leave them in the bedroom.

I wonder, then, where to place my note. The table in the living room is crowded with flowers, presents, cards. Last week Susan had a birthday party in a nearby restaurant. There must have been almost thirty guests. In her new denim dress and pretty shoes with flowers sewn on the sides, she rushed at each friend as they came in. There was kissing and hugging and shouted bits of gossip. Soon the floor was strewn with ribbon and wrapping paper. I sat and watched her dancing to Tamla Motown records with a school friend. They even danced nostalgically. I recalled a time I was in Venice. She was joining me at the Hôtel des Bains on the Lido, but I didn't know at what time. I had gone downstairs and saw her by accident in the lobby, and she turned and recognized me and her face was full of pleasure.

She's not my type at all, but I'm sure there is something about her I could enjoy. I would like not to see her for a few months, in order to forget her; perhaps, then, I could get a clear view of what she is like, apart from me.

I place the note at the other end of the table, leaning it against a cup. She will not miss it when she comes in. She will sit in that chair over there to read it. I wonder what she will feel then; I wonder what she will do then. The phone is at hand.

I pick up my bag from the centre of the bedroom floor. I walk downstairs and open the front door. Tired but determined, I step outside. It hasn't rained for weeks. The blossom is out. London is in bloom; even I am in bloom, despite everything.

It is a lovely day for leaving.

I shut the door behind me and walk away. I consider going through the park and seeing the boys. But my distracted demeanour would give me away and any questions could cost me the little courage I have. Perhaps I should turn and wave at the house.

I can't say I haven't learned more in this crucible than I've learned anywhere: the education of a heart, slightly cracked, if not broken in places. Whether I will survive the knowledge and put it to good use – whether any of us will – is another matter.

Victor is sitting at the table in his black dressing gown, black socks and slippers, chewing on a piece of toast left on the table from last night, no doubt. But when I come through the door he gets up and kisses me.

'It's done?'

'Yes,' I say. 'It is done.'

Victor watches me and looks jaunty. I notice that the flat has been cleaned. There is not a pickled onion in sight.

I consider unpacking, so as to make it clear to myself that I am staying. But looking around, I cannot see where I will put my things. He will leave for work later, and I will be here alone. I don't feel like going to the office. Perhaps I will go for a walk.

Victor takes my bag and puts it down in the corner. I notice that the coffee is fresh. There are croissants in the oven. I sit down and look at him, a friend. For a while – for how long I don't know – this place will be my home.

I wonder what time Susan will unfold the note and know, and know. She will not be back until the early evening. It is not too late to retrieve it.

'Did you know I'd come?'

'I thought you'd make it – eventually,' Victor replies. 'Perhaps in a few weeks. It had become inevitable.'

'You could tell?'

'How could I not?' Then he says, 'Have you told the kids?'

'No.'

'That is the hardest.'

I bite my lip.

'I'll speak to Susan first,' I say. 'Then them. I've got a lot to say to them . . . about the whole business of people trying to live together.'

He looks at me. He knows this. Still, he is unusually cheerful.

'What's making you smile?' I enquire.

'I have a new interest. We are having lunch in that new place, and then a walk in the park – '

'And then?'

His eyes shine.

He says, 'By the way, that girl rang.'

'Which girl?'

'Nina. She heard you were looking for her.'

I can only think of how good life on earth can be, at times. What grief two people can give one another! And what pleasure!

He says, 'I've written her number down in case you've forgotten it.'

'Thank you.'

He hands me the slip of paper. I pick up the phone and push the buttons; then I replace the receiver.

'Later,' I say. 'There will be time.'

We walked together, lost in our own thoughts. I forget where we were, or even when it was. Then you moved closer, stroked my hair and took my hand; I know you were holding my hand and talking to me softly. Suddenly I had the feeling that everything was as it should be and nothing could add to this happiness or contentment. This was all that there was, and all that could be. The best of everything had accumulated in this moment. It could only have been love.